CRAZY HAS A NAME

A NOVEL

NANCI LAMBORN

Crazy Has A Name: A Novel

Published by Bloomfire Press
Copyright © 2025 by Nanci Lamborn. All rights reserved.

ISBN: 979-8-218-57150-4
Christian Contemporary Fiction / Biographical Fiction

Cover design by Lisa Monias, copyright owned by Nanci Lamborn.

This novel is dedicated first to the Lord Jesus Christ, who has healed me in more ways than I can name; to each one of the living inspirations behind this story, for allowing me into your pain—I am so proud of all of you; and to my one-of-a-kind husband, who prayed every word into existence.

I also wish to acknowledge and thank Mike Hutchings of God Heals PTSD, whose groundbreaking work in inner healing prayer has brought healing and mental freedom to countless hurting people.

AUTHOR'S NOTE

This novel is inspired by true events and documented real-life miracles witnessed firsthand. As an inner healing and deliverance minister, I have had the privilege of working with thousands of individuals through profound journeys of emotional, spiritual, and physical healing. The story you are about to read weaves together authentic accounts of childhood trauma and supernatural transformation, drawn from the lives of multiple individuals I have encountered over the years.

While this story is inspired by several real people who experienced Jesus as The Healer in life-changing ways, their right to anonymity has led me to amend all names, places, and identifying details in this story.

It is my hope and prayer that Danny's journey will encourage, inspire, and remind you that complete freedom truly does exist. If, after reading, you are drawn to embark upon your own healing journey, please refer to the Resources page to take the next step.

With deep gratitude,
Nanci Lamborn

1

AGE FORTY-EIGHT

I was born in an insane asylum to a drug-addicted prostitute.

But right now I may punch someone in the face, or vomit all over the faded paisley rug. Perhaps both. This is probably not okay in a church therapy office. Since I'm a public high school counselor, neither would likely bode well for my reputation.

Marti, the lady across from me wearing the Christian fish necklace, unsettles me. She's nothing like other ministers or religious therapists I've met. She's real. She's funny. She's clearly knowledgeable and intelligent. My church friends Jim and Claudia recommended her. But why does she make me want to hide? We both claim to believe in Jesus Christ. What's with this sudden sweatiness from the simple question she asked?

"Danny," she starts, "will you tell me about the most painful memory connected to the woman you call Mom?"

The Others (the people only I can see and hear) don't like

her question. Kendra, one of the Others who is always recording my words on a clipboard, frowns and shakes her head. Garrison, the soldier in combat fatigues, squares his shoulders and locks his jaw. I close my eyes to keep from being distracted.

Deflection is necessary. "Haha, well, how much time do we have?" My voice is louder than intended. Hopefully this flashy smile covers the shakiness of my hands. I glance at my wife Grace as she sits angled toward me with a gentle hand on my knee. Her patient, tender expression encourages me as she nods, prompting me to continue. Sweat oozes from every pore, and I'm thankful for the air conditioning an overhead vent provides as it blows coolness across my neck.

A voice only I can hear, one of the Others who calls himself the Bossman, speaks up. "You've told the story a hundred times, Danny. You're fine. Man up."

Swallowing the rising lump in my throat and taking the familiar preparatory breath to separate from any vestige of feeling, I answer. "Well, Marti, if it's bad, I lived it. The locals called our area south of Lexington 'The Pit.' Some-body blew away my cousin in our front yard and we saw the aftermath. I was molested multiple times over the course of several years. My adoptive mom and my uncle were kind of like the gang leaders of the neighborhood, so they ran drugs and girls and whatever else they wanted. The cops were paid off, and—no surprise—they never came around. And from what they said more times than I can count, my folks paid two hundred dollars to buy me as a little kid in some kind of black-market ring in the foster system. They were all crazy. Me, too. But praise God, I'm different now! Jesus saved me as a dumb punk, although He hasn't really been around much the last few years... He must not care about the fact that I'm crazy. So I'm saved, but still a little crazy though!"

My laughter is once again too loud. The Bossman whispers, "See? Good job. You did fine."

Marti's brow furrows. "Wait a sec. You were literally bought for two hundred dollars? Isn't that trafficking?"

I shrug. "That's what we all call it today. This was back in the seventies, so it was more underground. But you must not have had much contact with the local foster care system. People with money will buy what they want, and they will always find a seller."

Marti leans in. Can her eyes peer into my soul?

"That's some super heavy stuff," she says. An uncomfortable pause follows as she studies me. "Has anyone ever asked you about the lack of emotion you express as you tell your story? Sometimes laughter is a mask for some incredibly deep pain."

Working in the public school system taught me how to answer without answering. Clearing my throat, I wipe imaginary dirt from my knee. "Ha, yeah, that's a good point. You're right about that." Garrison and Kendra both glare at me, but I look past them out the window behind Marti toward the sunshine. A late May breeze dances through the pink dogwood tree outside. Imagination has me sitting on a bench under that tree, looking up through the branches raining petals, enjoying the Kentucky springtime. Anywhere but in here.

Marti waits a few moments with a content smile. "You didn't actually answer my question," she says. How can words sound kind and scary at the same time?

Shrugging in silent defeat, I hold out my palms. Why did I let Grace bring me here? Can she sense my irritation?

Marti shifts in her seat and rests her notepad on one knee. "How about this?" she asks softly. "Let's start at the very beginning, with a complete family history."

If I look at Garrison and Kendra, the judgment and shame emanating from them will send me into a tailspin. Their discomfort with where this is going is palpable.

"Oh, boy," I say, clapping my hands and rubbing them together. "You buckled in? Okay then. Here we go!"

2

AGE FIVE

I'm almost six years old and I want to die. Or maybe I'm dead already.

My head hurts so bad, and there's a weird, thick taste in my mouth. Crud. Not dead. I'm lying in a heap at the bottom of the stairs. Again. Every part of me wants to cry, but they'll hurt me more if I do. I learned that a while ago.

If I keep my eyes closed long enough, the people won't kick me down the stairs anymore today. I decide to peek one eye half open. The foster daddy man, Mister Butch, and all of his friends are laughing. They point at me and say stuff to each other in words I don't know, and then they give each other money. The money thing makes no sense to me, but they do it whenever they kick me down the stairs. The one time I fell asleep after I hit the last step, they gave each other a lot of money after I finally woke up and started moving. Somehow the money is connected to my waking up, but I'm not sure how.

With one eye barely open and my cheek pressed to the

cold, hard floor, I see dirt and dust everywhere. A pair of heavy work boots Mister Butch dropped by the front door are all muddy, and some of the mud is stuck to the wall. A bug crawls in through the space under the door. I close my eye again.

A lighter clicks. Happy sounding words float by. A few moments go by and a sweet, sort of stinky smelling smoke fills the room. It's a little bit like cigarette smoke, but it's kind of like fruit that went bad and someone set it on fire. I don't know why, but slowly I start to feel dreamy and relaxed. I still hurt all over, but the smell of the smoke makes me not care about the pain.

Crud! I need to sneeze. They'll figure out I'm awake, but I can't help it. The sneeze hurts everywhere. For some reason, Mister Butch and his friends cheer when I sneeze. More money changes hands, and they turn their backs to me and click the lighter again. I take a long, deep breath that hurts so bad. But it seems like everything painful is finally over for today.

A board creaks from the top of the stairs, and I turn to find my big sister Danielle peeking around the hall corner. She says nothing, but she doesn't have to. Her face is all splotchy, but she is happy to see that I'm awake. She stretches her neck to make sure the grown-ups are busy, and she tiptoes down the stairs to me. With her mouth shut tight, she stares hard at me as she reaches under my back to lift me up. I squeeze my eyes because it hurts all over, holding my breath to keep from crying out.

My sister is a lot taller than me, so she puts me up onto her back. Trying not to make any noise, she carries me upstairs and into our room. She has found my stuffed elephant and my green lovey blanket in the closet and put them on my pillow for me. A sharp pain makes me jump a little as I lie back on the bed, and it takes a minute to lie all the way down. A wet washcloth is on the dresser by my bed, and Danielle lays it across my forehead once I'm still. A tear tries to come out of my eye, but I wipe it away, mad that I'm crying. Grabbing my lovey, I start to think again about what just happened, what always happens on the weekend in this house, but something breaks into my thinking.

"Danny, you don't have to take that anymore." A man's voice speaks to me. He talks nice, but he sounds strong. It hurts to open my eyes again, so I don't.

"What do you mean?" I ask. "Who are you?"

"My name is Garrison," he answers like a friend. "I'm here to help you so you don't have to feel the hurt anymore."

"Are you finding me a new family?"

"No, I can't do that," he says sadly. "But I have someplace you can go in your mind when they're mean to you."

Sharp fire shoots through my back, and I can't help but make noise under my breath as I turn onto my side toward the sound of Garrison's voice and open my eyes. I see a huge army soldier sitting on my floor with his legs crossed, looking right at me. He's dressed in a camouflage military jacket, matching pants, and heavy black boots. With his size, I bet he could toss my bed with one hand and beat up Mister Butch with the other hand at the same time. He should be scary, but somehow he's not.

"What does that mean?" I ask.

Danielle's chair squeaks as she turns toward me. "Who are you talking to?"

Garrison puts one finger up to his lips and holds it there as

7

he shakes his head side to side. Looking over my shoulder at Danielle, then back at the army guy, my eyebrows scrunch together in confusion. "You don't see an army man sitting here by me?"

In the middle of a yawn, Danielle rolls her eyes. "No, stupid! There's nobody in here but me and you. You were dreaming. Go back to sleep."

I turn back to Garrison. He says, "I'm not here for her. I'm here for you if you'll let me stay. She can't see me. Only you can see and hear me. This goes for everyone else, too. I'm *your* friend, Danny. I'm nobody else's friend." He scoots a little closer to me, and he reaches a ginormous hand to lay it gently over mine. "So you can't talk about me to anyone else because they'll call you crazy. Do you understand?"

Crazy. That's what they call my real mother Gypsy. "*Crazy has a name*," they say, then they laugh about her. I really don't want to be called crazy.

Garrison puts his hands together in his lap. As I look at him, his lips don't move, but his voice is loud and clear in my head. "It's our secret, Danny. Can you do that? Can you keep me a secret?"

I start to answer out loud, but I close my mouth and think of my words in my mind. "Why are you helping me?"

He smiles and answers, without moving his mouth. "Someone has to protect you from what those people are doing. I help people. That's my job, if you want."

"How do you..." I say aloud, and Garrison holds a finger to his lips again. I glance back at Danielle. She's bent over in her chair asleep with her head resting on her homework. Turning to look at him again, I start over in my head. "How do you do that? Help me, I mean."

He stands up to come and sit on the edge of my bed near my feet. "When they start to get mean, you just think about saying my name in your head. I'll let you take a nap at that point, and I'll take it from there. Then you'll just wake up when it's over. It's your choice if you want to think about me or not."

"That sounds easy," I say in my head. "I would like that."

Deep tiredness begins to take over, and I start losing the fight to keep my eyes open. Garrison makes me feel safer than I ever felt before.

I ask with my mind, "Will you stay here in case they come in while I'm sleeping?"

He stands up and takes a few big steps to the door, then he turns on one heel and gets straight and stiff, facing me. With his shoulders back, his chest out, and his jaw set, I think he looks like a real-life G.I. Joe. I want Garrison to be with me always.

I can sleep now. I am safe.

3

AGE FORTY-EIGHT

There's a light touch on my knee, and I can make out a voice. It's faint at first, then Grace's words get my attention.

"Danny." She squeezes my knee again. "Danny, want to come back with us?"

Like emerging from deep sleep, the present comes into focus as I regain my bearings. I take a cleansing breath and stretch. Where am I? Oh, right. We're in this church office with the ugly rug, with this woman who makes me nervous.

My cheeks grow hot at the realization of what just happened. I glance sidelong at my wife. "How long was I spaced out?"

She rubs my knee. "Not long, just a few minutes. Do you remember anything?"

Squeezing my eyes shut, I try to force something out of my brain, but there's only blackness. I glance at Garrison and Kendra. He frowns with his arms crossed, and she writes furiously on her clipboard as always. I blow out hard. "Nah, sorry, nothing," I say to Grace. "Just felt like I was asleep for a minute." I shake my head and sniff deeply. Looking back at Marti, I clear my throat. "My apologies; can you ask me that last question again?"

Marti picks up a small dry-erase board in one hand and grabs a marker with the other. "Let's try to draw out a family tree. Do you know your birth mother's maiden name?"

"Nicholson," I say. "Elizabeth Belle Nicholson, but she goes by Gypsy Belle."

"Is she still living?" Marti asks, brows raised.

"She is, actually, which is a shock given the lifestyle she led for so long. But she's not all there. She's in a memory care facility down in Franklin, Tennessee. The last time I saw her, she was delirious and heavily medicated, talking like I was a little boy. That's been something like fifteen, maybe eighteen years now. Haven't been able to bring myself to go back and see her." I shrug.

"I'm sorry," Marti says as she writes Gypsy's last name in the top left corner of the board. "And what do you know about your biological father?"

A bitter laugh escapes me. "Well, Gypsy was a prostitute, so we've got about half the population of Lexington as candidates. Supposedly right after she had me, there was one guy who had a thing for her, and he started claiming he was the father. From what I understand, he had money, and Gypsy just let everyone think it was him. They moved in together for a little while. Pretty sure his last name was Rawlins."

As Marti writes Rawlins on the board, a surprising flash of memory surfaces. "You know, now that we're talking about this question, I remember this one guy that came around a lot before they stuck me in foster care. I think they called him

Eddie. I remember getting a toy truck from him for my birthday once. It seems like Gypsy treated him differently, and we did have some similarities in the face. I always used to wonder if it was him."

Eddie's name goes on the board.

"Okay," Marti continues. "Before foster care, was there anyone else taking care of you on a regular basis? Any aunts or grandparents you remember?"

"No real family around, that's for sure," I answer. "Her mama died when Gypsy was about seven, and her daddy's family were bad people. I think she was already on the street at maybe thirteen, fourteen years old. But the lady who owned the brothel took care of me a lot. I never heard her real name, but she was called Big Nana. She was tough to everyone else, but she liked me for some reason. Maybe she felt sorry for me; I don't know."

Big Nana's name goes on the board.

"Now let's talk about the foster family," Marti says. "Were you only in one foster home, or did you move around?"

"Nope, just the one. The Blackwells. Butch and Gina Blackwell, and their sadistic redheaded son Carl Blackwell," I answer. "Wicked, evil family. Butch used to kick me down the stairs in front of his son and his brothers, and they would take literal bets on how long it would take for me to get up. That's not even the worst of it. They were some sick people, not just to me but to my sister, too. It's truly a miracle that I didn't die. It was absolute torture for over three years."

Marti adds their name to the board. "How were they able to stay in the foster care system?" she asks. "Seems like they'd eventually be caught."

"Not when your cousin is the DFACS supervisor and she's

sleeping with the chief of police." I laugh with my answer, but it doesn't feel funny. "Carl actually got certified as a foster parent as soon as he was old enough. That sicko kept hurting kids for years and nobody ever said a word."

"Ugh," says Marti. "The system is so broken." She holds up the whiteboard. "Okay, we have Nicholson, Rawlins, Eddie, Big Nana, and the Blackwells. You were adopted after a while, yes?"

I snicker again. "Well, you could call it that." Cynical anger pushes up from my belly.

Raising her eyebrows, Marti waits for more.

Taking a deep breath and plastering a smile, I ignore Garrison and Kendra's signals to stop. "Apparently there was an actual trafficking ring between that foster system and the local judge. So Roland Floyd Pierce and his wife Leona paid two hundred dollars to somebody, and I show up a month before my eighth birthday with adoption papers already signed. Roland complained all the time that he wasted two hundred dollars buying me. I can't count the number of times he told me he was looking for the receipt so he could return me to the people who sold me and get his money back." This story has crossed my lips many dozens of times, but today it stabs me in the heart.

Marti adds the name Pierce to the others on the board. "And this is the last name you've always maintained? Pierce?" she clarifies.

I lean back and straighten my sleeves. "Yeah. Once the pieces were all put together I prayed about changing it, but we've gone through a lot of work to redeem the last name, you know?"

"Makes sense," she nods. "Did they adopt your sister with you?"

I squeeze my eyes shut briefly to push away the aching sadness. "Nah," I answer. "She got adopted into a nice-looking home another county over at the same time I went to the Pierces. They looked like good people. I found out a few years ago that they even let her write letters to me. But I never saw them."

"I see," says Marti. "This Roland and Leona, the ones you ended up calling Mom and Dad, did they stay married?"

A scoffing growl escapes me. "Definitely not. I mean, they beat the snot out of me, they beat the snot out of each other. It was a circus." Betrayed by the shakiness of my voice, I force a cough. "Dad did not have it in him to stay faithful. They'd be okay for a while, all lovey-dovey. It was kind of gross actually. Then they'd both start drinking again, they'd beat each other up, then he would leave and be gone for maybe a month shacked up with somebody new. Mom would stay drunk for a few days and eventually come out of it mad as a hornet. But then I'd come home from school one day, and he'd just be sitting at the table with her running her fingers through his hair, like he'd never left. But yeah, they finally divorced when I was about fourteen, I guess."

"So what finally led to their divorcing for good?"

At this question, Garrison strides toward me and leans in, his face close to mine. A chill runs down my back at the bulging veins in his neck. "Not a word, Danny," he whispers through gritted teeth. He turns around and moves back beside Kendra.

I sigh and put on my best sheepish face. "That's a story for another time."

Marti doesn't press. She takes a lot of notes on her notepad as I speak. Every ink mark feels like evidence against me. Kendra does the same thing. But I'm used to her recording my life, so I don't look at her. My hands trembling, I lace my fingers together and squeeze until discomfort makes the tremor stop.

The Bossman speaks up again in my head. "Keep it together, man. It's all under control." Usually he's believable, but today he sounds like a smarmy salesman.

Marti's voice helps me focus. "Did either Roland or Leona ever remarry and bring a step-parent into the mix?"

My eyelids suddenly feel droopy and I stifle a yawn. I have no idea why I'm sleepy this early in the day. "She never got married again, but she would move a new boyfriend in about once every two years. Most of them were mean. I remember one of them locked me outside without a coat one night when it was snowing. And she was dealing big time, so all of the boyfriends were strung out while they used her for free dope."

Holding the whiteboard up on one knee, Marti turns it toward me as she reads each entry aloud. Every name identified in large, black letters all together brings a mixture of anger, grief, and sadness. My heart starts to race in the presence of emotion, and Garrison strides toward me again. He's not angry. He's in protector mode.

As Marti starts to mention something about praying over the bloodlines, heaviness begins to overtake me. Marti's voice fades as if muffled by a thick mist, and I find myself unable to resist as I slip into sweet nothingness.

4

AGE FIVE

I am five years old, and I have been made to do something very wrong.

Mister Butch seems tired of sharing money with his friends after kicking me down the stairs. The last time he got mad because I hit my head so hard that I went to sleep for a long time. Danielle says I was on the floor all afternoon. Miss Gina yelled at Mister Butch about me and then she had to pay money for a nurse to come to the house and take care of me. Miss Gina and Mister Butch had a huge scary fight. Carl is still awful mean to me, and Mister Butch still kicks me, but not down the stairs anymore.

Danielle and I have been visiting a playground around the corner. I like it there. Other kids my age talk to me and play with me, and no one is mean. Some of the boys talk about a place they go in the mornings to learn about colors and shapes and letters from a nice lady they call a teacher. The place they go is some kind of kid garden, but I don't know the word. No one reads to me in my house, so I do not read. Danielle has books from her school, and sometimes I look at the pictures in them and make up stories in my head about what the people in the pictures are doing. Garrison likes to sit with me when I tell the stories. He listens to me. No other grown-ups ever do.

Mister Butch and Carl have started to act weird. Since a few weeks ago, Carl looks at Danielle funny. He just stares at her whenever she walks through the house, running his hand through his thick, red hair, not saying anything. The way he looked at her made me afraid for Danielle, but I'm not sure why. He would smile as he watched her, but it wasn't a nice smile. His smile is like the mean smile from *How the Grinch Stole Christmas*.

Then Mister Butch started being near Danielle all the time. He would stand behind her while we were eating breakfast and play with her hair. She hated it. She would always look at me while Mister Butch ran his fingers through her hair, and she would squeeze her eyes shut. Then he would put his hands on her shoulders and tell her how cute she was and how all the boys wanted to marry her and stuff. She would be too scared to say anything, so she would just wait for him to stop. One time she was crying, but Mister Butch didn't see.

He never did that when Miss Gina was in the room.

Miss Gina has been gone a lot now. She used to stay home with us mostly, but now she says she has to go to work at a job because taking care of us costs a lot of money. She wasn't always very happy or nice, but she was way nicer than Mister Butch and Carl. She seems smiley and happy when she leaves for work. I wonder if she's happy because she doesn't have to take care of me and Danielle.

Last week Mister Butch had one of his friends over when we came downstairs for breakfast. I'd seen this man a few times before, laughing and passing money after I would wake up at the bottom of the stairs from being kicked. Mister Butch calls him Rocko. He never talks to us, only to Mister Butch.

Rocko is so ugly that he scares me. The skin on his face is all lumpy and scarred. When I had the chicken pox, it left little holes in the places where the chicken pox sores were. I think Rocko must have had chicken pox on his whole face.

He has a long and jagged raised line that goes from the corner of one eye down to his ear. It looks like a zipper. He also has some weird dark gray words and letters painted all around his neck and shoulders. There are some scary Halloween-looking faces in the paint, and things that must be words. He has the same kind of things painted on top of both of his huge hands, and he always has black stuff under his fingernails.

Last week Rocko came to breakfast again, and he had a big box with him. It had all kinds of black wires and cords sticking out of it. Mister Butch carried the box upstairs and put it on the floor outside of our room. I thought maybe they were giving us a TV of our own.

I was wrong.

That morning during breakfast, Rocko walked upstairs and started digging into the box, and he asked Carl to help him. Mister Butch told Danielle that he needed her to do something for him, and he said he needed me to help. He was being much nicer than usual.

I was excited that he wanted my help with something! Danielle did NOT seem excited.

Mister Butch took Danielle's hand and led her upstairs to our room. He told me to stay at the table until he called for me to help him. Smiling as I ate, I patiently waited for the chance to be the helper.

When he finally called down the stairs, I took two stairs at a time.

"I'm ready to help!" I said, running into our room. It was so bright in there, at first I thought I had gone in the wrong door. I didn't understand why there were a bunch of lamps from around the house that were on in our room.

I saw Carl and Rocko just inside the door standing behind a big black square thing that sat on top of three tall metal sticks that went all the way to the floor. The black square thing had a cord plugged into the wall, and there were several buttons and tiny glowing lights on it. Rocko was pressing some of the buttons and moving the black thing around.

The black square thing had a part on the front of it that looked like something one of the boys had brought to the playground a few days ago. He'd called it a telescope. Rocko leaned in close to the back of the square thing and put his eye right up to a big hole. He pressed another button that made a beep and told Mister Butch that his camera was all set.

Then I saw Danielle lying on top of her bed. But where were her clothes? She must have been so cold! Her face was red and splotchy.

Mister Butch grabbed my hand and leaned down to come face to face with me. His eyes were squinty and he looked at me like I had just wet the bed again. He smelled like cigarettes and stinky armpit.

"Danny-boy," he said, his voice low and scary. "You and your sister are going to help me with something. You are going to do exactly as you are told, and you will not tell anyone. Ever. If you disobey me, I will hurt you, and then I

will hurt your sister, and it will be your fault. Do you understand me?"

I nodded, too scared to even open my mouth. Then
Garrison walked into the room.

Mister Butch led me by the hand over to my sister. He said
I had to take off my clothes and lay next to her, and then I had
to do exactly as he instructed.

As Garrison walked toward me, I started to feel better as
everything faded away to sleeping black.

Waking up awhile later to more beeping from the black
square thing Mister Butch called a camera, I see Carl take off
his Yankees baseball hat and run his hand through his thick
red hair to get it up off of his forehead as he tells Mister Butch
they're done. Done with what? And why am I lying here
beside my sister? Then Mister Butch starts unplugging the
lamps as Rocko and Carl take apart the black metal sticks and
return everything to the box and leave the room.

Now I realize my clothes are on the floor, and I have done
something very, very wrong.

I cannot look at Danielle as she jumps off of her bed and
throws her clothes on. She cries hard as she runs down the
stairs and out the side door. I think maybe she's going to walk
to school, but she's left her schoolbooks on her desk.

My green lovey blanket and stuffed elephant invite me to
run to my bed and cover up. I'm not sure what to do but just
lay here under my lovey. My body shakes and I can't stop it,
and I think I might want to throw up. Garrison isn't here
anymore.

"What have you done, Danny-boy?" A lady's voice makes
me jump.

Looking toward the voice, I see a woman standing by the

open door. Her hair is all twisted up into a ball on the top of her head, and she wears ugly black eyeglasses. She has a pile of papers clipped on a wooden board resting in one elbow and a pen in the other hand. She looks meaner than the wicked witch of the west.

I start to shake and cry, and my tummy starts doing flips. *What have I done?!*

"This is your fault, you know," she says as she writes, her voice hard and sharp like a whip. "This will have to go on your permanent record."

Permanent record?! I remember the mean man at the courthouse saying something about a permanent record, and I think Miss Gina told Danielle that getting into trouble at school goes onto her permanent record. I don't know what a permanent record is, but it must be bad. I cry even harder.

Looking down at me from over her glasses, the lady stops writing. "Good little boys don't behave like this, Danny. Do you want to be a bad little boy or a good little boy? From what I see, you are not a good little boy."

Sniffing and wiping my nose on the back of my hand, I have a hard time making words come out. "I... I want to be good." My voice squeaks like a mouse.

She smiles, happy with my answer. "My name is Kendra," she says as she slides her pencil over one ear and holds her papers to her chest. "My only job is to make sure that you behave like a good little boy should. I will be keeping very clear notes about absolutely everything you do. Someone has to make sure that the list of naughty things is smaller than the list of good things. That is how I can be sure that you are a good little boy."

My cheeks turn bright red as a heavy sense of wrongness and badness washes over me. "Are you going to tell anyone?"

Taking a deep breath, she smiles, but her eyes are still mean and scary. "Garrison knows that I'm here. He already knows everything. But I will have no choice but to tell other people if the things on the naughty list continue." Spinning around, she stomps out of my room.

She can see and hear Garrison, too.

5

AGE SEVEN

I am almost eight years old, and some people just bought
me. I'm not sure what that means. I'm not a toy on a shelf
in a store.

Early this morning Miss Gina had banged on our bedroom
door to wake up me and Danielle. It's not a school day, so we
weren't sure what was happening. Miss Gina rushed in with
two trash bags in her hand, way more mad than she usually
was.

"Get up," she ordered. "Pack your stuff. You're moving.
Someone is waiting for you downstairs. You can't have the
sheets or the toothpaste. You have ten minutes."

Danielle and I looked at each other for a second, and we
both started to smile when we realized what this meant.

We were finally leaving this horrible place!

Kendra was in the corner like normal, but I didn't care. I
was moving!

We couldn't grab things fast enough. Neither one of us
ever had a lot of stuff to begin with, so fitting it all in one

trash bag each wasn't hard. Carrying the full bag was heavier than I thought, and I just dragged it clunking down the stairs behind me.

A big, sweaty, unsmiling lady in a brown suit stood just inside the front door. She had her own picture in a square piece of plastic stuck to her suit near her neck, and she had two paper folders under her arm. She watched me clunk my trash bag down the stairs, but she didn't offer to help. She just stared.

When Danielle came up behind me with her much fuller trash bag, the sweaty lady opened the front door and jerked her head toward the outside. As Danielle and I started to walk out the door, we saw Mister Butch and mean Carl sitting in the living room watching TV. As they looked in our direction, I saw Danielle hold up just the middle finger of her hand in their direction. I don't know what that means, but it must be a kind of joke because Mister Butch laughed. Danielle didn't laugh back. Carl just pulled his Yankees baseball cap from his hands, ran his hands through his thick red hair, and looked back to the TV.

Hustling outside, we saw that the unsmiling lady had opened the back doors of an ugly gray Ford Falcon with rusted bumpers. She sat in the driver's seat with the car already running. Danielle had to help me get my trash bag up into the car and close my door. Her door wasn't even shut all the way before the lady was backing out of the driveway.

I was so glad to see Garrison sitting in the front seat. He was coming too!

We drove for a while. The lady smoked cigarette after cigarette with her window only open a tiny crack as she wiped her dripping face with a hand towel. She had the car radio station tuned to some really old, boring music. I watched out the window mostly, but whenever I looked up to face the front windshield, the sweaty lady was glaring at us in the mirror.

My stomach made funny noises.

They forgot to give us breakfast!

"I'm hungry," I said to the sweaty lady.

"Zip it, boy!" the lady barked. She took another long puff of a cigarette. "I ain't your personal chef. The people who bought y'all can deal with feeding y'all. You can wait until you get to your new houses."

Bought us? I didn't know we were for sale.

For now, Danielle and I just shrug at each other. I find my lovey blanket and my stuffed elephant in the top of my trash bag and pull them close.

Not much later, the car pulls into a tree-lined, shady driveway. Danielle and I try to sit up tall to see where we are. A nice-looking red brick house with a wooden swing on the front porch comes into view. We both smile big at each other. I imagine us playing kickball in the front yard grass, and swinging together on the porch while we sing "Old MacDonald."

As the sweaty lady stops the car, she honks the horn and opens her door. Her feet on the driveway, she leans in through her door to face the back seat and point at me.

"You're staying there, boy," she says. "This is your sister's new house, not yours." She slams the front door.

Danielle is almost out of the car now, and her eyebrows scrunch together. "Wait, what?" she asks as she looks back at me. "You're splitting us up?! You can't do that!" Now she's crying hard as she reaches out to try to grab me. "Danny!"

The lady pushes Danielle out of the way and slams the

back door shut. Grabbing Danielle's elbow, she drags my sobbing sister toward the pretty house. Danielle continues to scream my name and point at me.

I holler and cry, too. "Don't take my sister away! Danielle! Nooooo!" I kick and hit against the door, and I try hard to open it, but I can't unlock it.

My face pressed against the dirty window, I see the sweaty lady pull Danielle to the house where a man and lady stand at the bottom of the porch steps, smiling really big. They can't hear me, but I cry and scream anyway.

The happy lady squats down and opens her arms up to my sister. Scooping her up in a big bear hug, she turns and carries Danielle, still crying hard, up the stairs and into the nice brick house. The happy man pulls his wallet out of his pants pocket, takes out some money, and gives it to the sweaty lady. She gives him one of the paper folders she'd been holding earlier. Picking up Danielle's trash bag, he turns and follows his wife into the nice, shady house.

My sister is gone.

Hugging my lovey blanket tighter, I turn back to Garrison. He's backward in the front seat now, facing me, and I can't help falling into a dark sleep.

The slam of a car door shakes me awake. I forgot where I was until I see the inside of the dirty gray car and my trash bag on the seat beside me. My heart hurts so bad.

My sister is gone.

I almost start crying again, but my door flies open and the sweaty lady yells at me. "Let's go, boy. Time to meet your new mommy and daddy."

Giving me barely a second to get my trash bag, my lovey, and my elephant, the sweaty lady grabs my elbow. She walks fast, and I have to try hard to keep up with her. She had parked the ugly gray car right along the curb in the street, and I didn't see a driveway at any of the houses here. I do see a bunch of cars parked along the street. One of them is sitting up on big concrete blocks. One car doesn't have a hood to cover the engine. Another has two flat tires and a broken window. Three older, skinny boys sit on the hood of that car smoking cigarettes.

My mouth drops open as I see the house we're walking toward. All of the houses along this street are connected, with no yard or alley between them. Each house has its own front porch, and the steps from the porch come right down to the sidewalk. There's not much open space, just house after house. It's all so nasty and dirty.

The roof over the porch is kind of sagging to one side. The house we're walking toward is mostly a gross yellowish color, but lots of the paint is peeling off and it's a gray color underneath. If it was nighttime at Halloween, this would be a haunted house.

Railing pieces run along the front of the raised porch, but some of the pieces are broken and hanging down. Some pieces are just gone, and there are holes and ragged pieces of wood sticking out every which way. The porch steps are concrete, but they're all cracked and crooked. The houses on each side of this house have small fences with gates at the steps, and the fences and gates are all crooked and broken. I see a few pieces of white wood that must have been a whole fence for this ugly yellow house a long time ago, but there's no gate. One of the upstairs windows has cardboard taped over it.

There are no trees or grass anywhere. Just concrete steps,

sidewalk, bare brown dirt, and the street. A dog barks from somewhere close by, sounding large and scary.

Garrison stays right next to me as the sweaty lady walks me up the broken concrete stairs onto the porch. She goes so fast I almost drop my trash bag. There's a metal screen door with half the screen part all torn up. The sweaty lady opens it and pounds on the front door. "Roland!" she yells. "The boy's here!"

Scooting closer to Garrison, I hear thudding footsteps coming from inside the yellow house. The front door creaks open a second later. Seeing me and the lady, the man squeezes through the door to come outside. He wears a torn tank top and oil-stained blue jeans, and I see some of the same dark blue painted pictures on his arms that I saw painted on Rocko. He stares down at me with a cigarette hanging from his mouth. He is not smiling or happy.

"So this is what two hundred dollars gets me, huh?" he asks the sweaty lady.

She pushes me toward the unhappy man. "Danny, this is your new father," she says. "His name is Roland Pierce, but you will call him Dad. Your name is now Danny Pierce because he has adopted you. You live here now. Do you understand?"

I definitely do not want to live here.

I look at Garrison. I'm so glad he's here. He doesn't look afraid. He looks strong.

As I start to nod with a yes, I jump as I hear a super loud pop sound, almost like someone had set off fireworks right behind the house. But it was the middle of the daytime, so it couldn't be fireworks. Right after the pop sound, I hear some people yelling at each other. My eyes grow wide and I fight the tears that want to come.

"Wilson!" this man I'm supposed to call Dad yells toward the street, much louder than I expected. "Knock it off, man!"

The yelling people start to quiet down as Dad pulls a fist-sized roll of money from his pocket. "Man, that guy's lost it," Dad says as he counts out some of the money and hands it to the sweaty lady. "He don't quit the dope, he's gonna get his self or somebody else killed, know what I'm sayin'?"

She gives Dad the other paper folder she'd been holding. Looking at the papers inside, he asks her, "There a receipt in here in case I need to return him?"

The sweaty lady rolls her eyes and turns back toward the concrete stairs. Before she reaches the bottom, out of nowhere a green muscle car comes speeding up the street. Its back windows are open, and a tall, creepy looking man leans out the window looking back down the street. I see a small black gun in his hand. Tires squeal and a dog starts barking crazy. A second later, those three older, skinny boys come running up the street as fast as they can go. They're yelling something mean about getting to the people in the green car. One of them holds a gun, too.

Dad laughs at the look on my face. It's not a nice laugh. He pushes the front door all the way open.

"Welcome to The Pit, kid. Don't make me ask that lady for my money back."

6

AGE NINE

I am nine years old, and I'm inside the bottom kitchen cabinet between the oven and the sink. It smells weird in here.

The crack at the edge of the cabinet door brings in just enough light to notice the moldy, wet corner under the sink pipes. I catch something moving to my right, and I count three small roaches hurrying into the gap around the drainpipe. My knees are shoved up under my chin, and my arms are wrapped around my knees to hold them still so I don't accidentally push the cabinet door back open.

Mama and Dad are killing each other. At least that's what it sounds like.

Mama started it this time. She was already drunk when Dad came home from work late, and the dinner she had made him was cold and stale. Mama said something about a red lipstick stain on his shirt collar, and things blew up. I guess they both forgot I was sitting at the dinner table. Dad came rushing toward Mama and pushed her backward over the table, food and dishes flying everywhere. I couldn't get around them to run up to my room, so I slid down from my chair and climbed in here to wait it out.

I can't help crying. All of the yelling and the crashing makes me jump, and I press my hands over my ears. It doesn't help much. The noise of them hurting each other starts to make my tummy hurt. I might throw up. I hear the zipping sound of Dad's belt being yanked from his pants, and Mama yelps as the belt hits her with a crack. I get all goose bumply as I remember how the belt stings, and I cry harder as snot runs down my face onto my knee.

When I grow up, I will never, ever be like them!

"You're fine, Danny," says an unkind male voice. I lift my hands from over my ears, but I only hear the fighting. I cover my ears again and squeeze my eyes shut, then I hear the voice again. "They've done this before and it always stops eventually. Quit being such a baby."

Who could be saying that?

"I'm a friend," says the voice. He sure doesn't sound friendly. *Wait, he heard the words I'm thinking in my mind!* "Yes, Danny," he replies, still annoyed. "I can hear the words in your mind. I'm in here with you." I think if I had an older brother and he was mad at me, this voice is what he would sound like. Only I don't have an older brother, and I'm hearing this in my head while my parents tear up the house.

"You can call me The Bossman," the voice says. "If you listen to me, you'll be fine. If you don't, then you'll just be this crying little baby hiding in the cabinet."

Sweat starts to run down my back. I sniff hard and wipe my wet nose and eyes on my shirt sleeve. "Why are you here?" I ask aloud quietly.

The Bossman shushes me. "You don't have to talk out loud to answer me!" He seems mad. "I already told you I can hear your thoughts. And I'm helping you because, duh, obviously you need help right now, and no one else is here. Garrison isn't here. I don't know where Kendra went."

He knows about the Others!

"Yes," the Bossman says with a weary sigh. He must not like me very much. "Garrison comes around when you're in real danger, and Kendra writes down all of the bad stuff that you do. But like I said, you're fine. Your parents will get tired soon. They'll stop fighting, and then you can go to bed."

Someone falls hard against my cabinet door and cries out in pain. I jump again. Whoever it was gets right back up. I hear a sharp crash and a crackling, buzzing sound. My shoulders drop as I guess that our only television is now in pieces. *Great.*

"It's fine, Danny. Your dad will steal another one like he always does. Stop worrying about it like a little baby."

I'm NOT a baby! Stop calling me that. Angry tears start up again.

"Then stop acting like one," he snaps.

Then what am I supposed to do in here? It's gross.

"Think about someplace fun that you like to go, and let the movie screen in your mind play like you're actually there." The Bossman's attitude toward me seems nicer now.

I think about the King's Island park in Cincinnati. Uncle Mickey takes me there at least twice a year. My favorite ride is the Scooby Doo coaster. Uncle Mickey let me ride it ten times in a row last year.

The movie screen of my mind plays the roller coaster ride, and I begin to relax. I love being in the very front car, so I think about riding on a sunny summer day. I begin to hear the sound of the track chain as it slowly pulls the string of cars up the wooden hill, clicking and shaking as it climbs. I can even smell the popcorn and cotton candy and hot black pavement all mixed together, and I see myself smiling as the red and yellow ride crests the top of the first hill. My stomach drops a little as I remember what it feels like to be flying down the first bumpy hill, the air rushing past and messing up my hair as I laugh. Around the first curve and down a smaller hill, my body moves with the hills and dips as the coaster flies up and down and up again. Another curve, another small hill, another curve, and we race to the end where the car jerks to a stop. *What a ride!*

"Wanna ride again?" asks the Bossman. I don't have to answer as the ride resumes in my mind. This time, the tinkly sound of music is playing through the park speakers, and I can almost feel the metal bar across my lap and the hard seat under me bouncing as I ride. Then I think about riding again on a warm, dark summer night with all of the lights flashing. From the very top of the first hill, I look around at the rest of the park, all lit up like a Christmas carnival. My mouth waters a little at the smell of hot dogs and funnel cakes, and I am so happy. Then I think about some of the other rides in the park, and I imagine riding The Flying Dutchman, the Spinning Keggers, Halley's Comet, and The Rotor. But I go back to the Scooby-Doo coaster between each of those.

I don't know how long I spend riding the rides at King's Island. By the time I decide I've had enough riding, I realize I am in the dark, and the house is totally quiet.

"Told ya," whispers the Bossman.

I slide out of the cabinet onto the kitchen floor. I've been under there so long, my bottom is asleep, and my back and legs hurt. Light from a streetlamp shines through the kitchen window, and I see holes and broken things everywhere. I start to walk across the kitchen floor, and something sharp stabs the bottom of my bare foot. Sucking in my breath at the pain, I pick up my left foot and pull the sharp thing out and toss it away. I can't walk through here barefooted. I step up onto the nearest dining room chair, and I hop and climb from chair to table and to another chair until I'm close enough to the stairs to jump.

Tip-toeing up the far right side of the staircase where the squeaks in the floor are the softest, I make it upstairs and quietly open and close my bedroom door.

I'm so tired I can barely stand up, but I'm not scared anymore. Without changing my dirty clothes, I crawl into bed. My old, green lovey blanket is still folded up under my pillow where I left it, and I pull it close to me in the dark.

"See, Danny," the Bossman says quietly. "You're just fine."

I'm just fine. Will you be here tomorrow?

"If you want me to," he answers. He sounds even nicer now. "I can be here whenever you think things are going bad, and I'll remind you to ride the roller coasters in your mind until things blow over, and you'll be fine."

Yes. I'll be fine.

7

AGE TEN

I am ten years old, and I'm standing outside in the spot where my favorite cousin was shot dead.

Yesterday had been like any other day in The Pit. Mama and Uncle Mickey had been in some hush-hush talks for a few hours in the morning. It sounded like things got heated a couple of times. That was normal. I knew better than to ask any questions. But this meeting was way longer than usual, and they both left real mad.

The less I know about what they do with dope and money, the better.

Uncle Mickey and Mama run the neighborhood like people in *The Godfather* movie we saw a few months ago. Mama and Uncle Mickey aren't in a gang, but the gangs around here do whatever they say. I'm sure there's guns and dope involved.

Nobody messes with Mama.

One day last month I came home from school to a visitor. I knew someone had stopped by because there was an unfamiliar rusty orange bicycle leaned up against the porch. I opened the front door quietly and went straight up the stairs toward my room. I knew better than to ever interrupt anybody visiting Mama.

About halfway up the stairs, I heard a man crying. I turned around on the step, trying not to make a sound, and I peeked my head over the handrail where I could just see part of the kitchen table. Mama's hands were visible up to the elbow, but the rest of her was out of sight behind the wall.

Mama had a gun under her hands on the table.

There was a skinny older man sitting right across from her at the part of the table I could see. His clothes were a little dirty, but I don't think he was homeless. He was taller than Mama, but his shoulders were hunched way over and his head hung down. His arm and neck were covered in tattoos. He was balding on the top with wispy, grayish black curls above his ears. A dark purple bruise just above his left ear looked pretty fresh, and there was a stack of cash on the table in front of him.

He was the man sobbing.

He'd been crying so much I could see snot hanging off his nose. A box fan blew the smell of Mama's stale coffee and menthol cigarette smoke through the room.

I lowered myself down without a sound to sit on the stair. Mama talked in a low voice like I'd never heard before.

"Come on now, Benny," she said. "How long you been my customer, hmm? You know the drill, man." Mama's voice wasn't raised, but she didn't have to yell. The tone was terrifying enough.

"You know I'm good for it, Miss Leona," he answered, squeaking a little as he reached up to gently touch the bruise over his ear. "Some kids jumped me after a deal last night. They's the ones got the rest of your cash. I swear I just gotta find 'em is all. Please."

"Like I said, Benny. You bring Michelle over here tonight at eight-thirty. Then you can come back and get her tomorrow night. Then we're square. That's the deal."

"But, Miss Leona," he begged, "she's only fourteen! She ain't caught up in none of this stuff. She's a good girl." He lifted his chin to look straight at Mama, tears streaming. "I'll work for you for free. I'll run whatever you want me to run. Her older brother is already crossways with me. If I bring her here and he finds out…"

Mama cut him off by snatching up her gun and pointing it straight at his head. "Is that a threat?!" she barked.

The broken man in front of her dropped his head as he raised both hands in a half-hearted defense. "No, ma'am," he whispered. "I'd never threaten you, ma'am."

Mama laid the gun down and pulled Benny's pile of cash across the table to her side. "I make sure everybody knows the terms up front, Benny. I was never unclear with you. But I do thank you for being honest with me."

Mama stood, her chair scraping the floor. I slipped up the stairs and ducked into my room, pushing in on the door so it would latch without any noise. I spread some books and my composition paper across the bed, flipped on my transistor radio, grabbed a pencil and climbed belly down onto the bed. I was three spelling test repetitions in when Mama knocked and opened the door.

I jumped more than I thought I would.

"Didn't know you were up here," she said, taking a long

drag on a fresh cigarette. "Didn't hear you come in the house."

Keeping my eyes on my paper, I shrugged. "I don't know how you didn't see me. I came in through the front door like I always do. I'm hungry. Do we have anything to eat?"

I could feel her staring, but I didn't budge. After several moments, she took another long drag and turned to leave. "There's a box of cereal on the counter and a quart of milk in the fridge."

I was scrambling toward the kitchen before she could finish. As I did, Mama started pulling the sheets off of my bed. "I need you to go stay at Uncle Mickey's house tonight. I'm having some guests over, and they'll need the bed."

I clapped my hands together. A sleepover on a school night! With my cousin Frankie!

Frankie was sixteen, but he never treated me like I was a little kid. He could already drive a car, and he'd take me with him and his friends whenever they would go cruising or hanging out. I never told Mama, but he even let me drive a few times.

He was gonna be somebody, and he knew it. Sure, he sold dope. Lots of people did. But everybody loved Frankie. He could talk all businesslike and mature. He looked so grown, he could get into any bar in Lexington without having to use his fake ID. I knew he knew how to fight. He put a couple boys in the hospital before he turned thirteen. He even taught me a few moves. But he wasn't mean like Dad or Mama or Uncle Mickey. Even if Frankie was spitting mad, it never showed. He was cool as a cucumber.

Mama had guests who needed my bed a few more times after that. I never cared that other people slept in my room.

Mama always put clean sheets on the bed. Plus they always had food at Frankie's house.

I was supposed to sleep at his house again last night. But right after the streetlights came on, Uncle Mickey got a phone call. Frankie was teaching me how to play poker at the kitchen table when Uncle Mickey slammed the phone down.

"There's trouble at Leona's," he called to Frankie as he pulled on his leather bomber jacket that always had two loaded handguns concealed inside. "We gotta get over there right now." Letting the screen door slam behind him, Uncle Mickey peeled off on his Harley.

"Go get in the back seat, kiddo," Frankie said. "You keep your head down and don't ask no questions."

I scrambled into the car and sat on the back floorboard. I wasn't sure what "trouble at Mama's" meant. I thought maybe the sink was broken. But why would we need guns for that?

Frankie raced the two blocks over to his best friend Gino's house. The smell of fried chicken, cigarette smoke, and motor oil struck my nose as Gino jumped in and slammed the door.

"You ready?" Frankie asked, speeding back toward Mama's

The cocking of a nine-millimeter echoed in the car. "Ready," Gino answered.

Garrison sat in the back seat behind Frankie, watching straight ahead with his arms crossed. I was so glad he was there with me.

Shutting off the car's headlights, Frankie parked three houses up from Mama's. He looked back at me and said, "You stay here and I mean it. You got it?"

I could only nod. As the dome light came on inside the car

when Frankie and Gino opened their doors, the gold watch on Frankie's wrist glinted briefly in the light.

Cranking the back window all the way down after they left, I got up onto my knees in the back seat and leaned a little out the window. I could already hear yelling at Mama's.

A huge older boy was standing in the dust in front of Mama's porch. He was a lot taller than Frankie, and huge muscles bulged out from under his grimy white tank top. Uncle Mickey stood at the bottom of the porch steps, and Mama was on the top step smoking a cigarette. She leaned back against the corner post like she was watching kids play hopscotch.

Muscle Boy was loud. "What do you mean, pimping my sister? What's wrong with you people?! Michelle!" He cupped his hands toward my house and yelled her name again.

Uncle Mickey answered, "This ain't your business, boy. You need to get on back home. This don't concern you."

"Whatcha mean it ain't my business?" Muscle Boy answered. "I'm makin' it my business, 'cause ain't nobody else lookin' out for her. You got no right to do this! Michelle!" He started toward Uncle Mickey, but he didn't get very far before Uncle Mickey pulled both hands from his jacket, a handgun in each. Muscle Boy stopped, his hands up. Frankie and Gino sprinted up on either side of him, their guns aimed at his head.

My eyes wide, I glanced over at Garrison. "Whoa! You seeing this?" I whispered.

Uncle Mickey's voice boomed. "I said this ain't your concern, boy! Now you get off my street and we better not see you around here again. You mind your business."

Muscle Boy backed into the street. He picked up the rusty

orange bicycle that was lying on the curb and pedaled off into the night. After a minute everybody put their guns away, and Mama disappeared back into the house. Frankie, Gino, and Uncle Mickey huddled up to talk, then Gino jogged in my direction and climbed into the driver's seat.

"Hey kid, I'm taking you back to your uncle's house. Mickey and Frankie are gonna stay here at your mom's for awhile just in case the guy comes back. But you gotta get in bed in Frankie's room. Understand?"

I started to protest, but one sideways look from Gino shut me up. "They'll be there when you wake up for breakfast in the morning," he promised.

This morning I heard that Gino broke his promise because Frankie didn't come home.

I guess the muscle boy went and got his own gun. He'd waited a little while and then he and a friend hot-wired a car and drove back toward Mama's house with the lights off. Frankie had been standing down in the dust while Uncle Mickey had gone into the house. The driver of the car sped up Mama's street with Muscle Boy hanging out the back window, and Frankie never stood a chance.

Now I stand here in the dust, blood still spattered everywhere. My favorite cousin is gone, and I'm alone. A hot mad rush like I never felt starts to rise up from in my belly. Unsure what else to do, I sit on the bottom porch step and pick up pebbles to throw. Before the first one hits the ground, I sense someone over my left shoulder.

"Hi, Danny," a boy says. "I'm Brody."

He reminds me of Frankie with way bigger muscles. I wonder why I've never seen him before when he knows my name.

He sits beside me on the step. "You're right," he says. "You've never seen me before. You didn't need me until today."

He can hear my thoughts just like the Others do.

"Yes, I can," Brody says. He picks up a pebble and throws it. "You mad?"

The inferno in my belly grows. "What do you think?" I snap.

"Wanna do something about it?" He throws another pebble, and it hits the mailbox across the street.

"Like what? I'm a skinny little kid. Nobody listens to me. What am I supposed to do about it?" As I reach for another pebble beside the porch, something shiny catches my eye. I reach down and pull a gold watch from the rubble. It has blood on it.

Frankie's watch.

I can barely control the fiery hate that rushes through me, and I start to tremble. My eyes narrow, my jaws clench, and my heart races. But I feel oddly sleepy at the same time.

As Brody stands up and cracks his knuckles, a sneaky, somewhat scary grin comes across his face. As I slip help-lessly into a dark void, Brody tips his chin in my direction. "See ya later, Danny."

8

AGE THIRTEEN

I am thirteen years old, and a cute girl in my homeroom class at school likes me. Her name is Amber. Thinking about her makes me sweaty and red-faced. I think I like her, too. She has long, jet-black hair, and she keeps it brushed all to one side to show off her row of ear piercings.

She doesn't seem to notice the times that I just want to hide under my denim jacket all day at school. If she does notice, she doesn't judge me. I've seen her hiding in her jacket sometimes, too.

I hate school, but I hate home more. I know there is food and water at school every day. That's more than I can say about home. When Dad is gone for more than a couple of weeks, Mama forgets to buy groceries and pay the water bill. Like this morning, the only thing in the refrigerator was a dried-out box of leftover fried rice. It tasted nasty, but I was hungry. She never forgets to buy her whiskey and cigarettes, though. I hate being hungry all the time.

Amber knows who my other friends are. I guess everyone

calls my friend group the stoners or the potheads, but we don't care. At least if someone needs a hit, they know exactly who to ask. Amber splits her time between hanging with the stoners, the goths, and the metalheads. For the most part, we all get along. She doesn't smoke, but she doesn't judge anybody.

She is so easy to talk to. Other girls seem all snooty and worried about their eyelashes and their expensive name-brand handbags. Amber is different. She's a lot smarter than she lets on to teachers, but I get that. No kid wants a teacher to turn you into the class nerd just because you're smart. I have never been all that good at school, but Amber helps me understand things better without making me feel stupid.

Mama is in full-on crazytown. I try to not be around or pay attention, but the last several months have been the worst I can remember. It's been over four months since I've seen or heard from Dad. That last fight before he left was so bad, the neighbors called the cops. No one ever calls the cops here. I have no idea where he went.

As usual, Mama had spent that first week completely plastered. Then she started acting weird. She started fixing her hair and wearing makeup. She cleaned up around the house. I heard her on the phone in the middle of the night, and she actually giggled. A few times, she stayed out all night long without ever calling me. I don't care; it makes things better for me when she's not around.

Then about two months ago, it all began to make sense as she introduced me to her new friend Curtis. I had come home from school early because of some teacher planning meeting, and there they were drinking coffee at the dining room table together. Mama had seemed flustered at first. But she'd composed herself and introduced me.

He stood up smiling and came over to me with his hand extended. This man wanted to shake my hand. No man had ever offered to shake my hand before. Eyeing him for a moment, I shook his hand.

"Pleased to meet you, son," he said. He towered over me, but I didn't feel afraid of him. His voice was tender, and he was dressed in slacks and a sport coat. This guy was nothing like my dad, or any of the other people Mama usually hung around with. I could tell he was classy. I wonder how he ended up with my mother.

Curtis let go of my hand and placed his hands into his pants pockets. "Listen, I think your mom and I are going to be spending time together, so that means I'll be around." I glanced at Mama. She made it awkward. "Maybe," he continued, "if you want, we could shoot a few hoops outside sometime."

My cheeks felt hot. "Yeah, maybe," I mumbled. No man had ever offered to shoot hoops with me before. "I gotta go do my homework. Nice to meet you."

Clearly, Curtis is Mama's new boyfriend. I had wondered if maybe Mama and Dad were finally getting a divorce, but I knew better than to ask.

True to his word, Curtis has been hanging around several days off and on since we met. Last month he even stopped by while Mama was gone, and we played a quick game like he had offered. It was actually fun. He didn't let me win, but he didn't blow a fuse when I beat him. Garrison came to stand at the front corner of the house a few times during the game, but he never said anything.

Curtis even asked me about any girls who were in the picture for me. I told him a little bit about this one who's extra special. I didn't mention her name, but I talked about how she treated me and how she made me feel strong and special. Thankfully he didn't make it weird. He was pretty cool about it. He's easy to talk to, and he remembers what I say. Mama and Dad never remember anything.

I didn't tell him that Amber and I were planning to sleep together.

This morning on the bus ride to school, I'm secretly hoping Curtis and I get to shoot hoops again after school. No one ever tells me their plans, so hopefully I'll find out when I get back home. Curtis is the polar opposite of any adult I've ever been around. He's educated, he dresses like a banker, and he doesn't talk to me like he's dealing with an annoying little kid. Mama is nicer to me when Curtis is around. I'm starting to wonder if maybe Mama and Curtis might get married. I'd be cool with that.

I also can't wait to see Amber again. Yesterday she pulled me behind the gym equipment door and we'd had a hot and heavy moment. The memory has played over and over in my mind nonstop since.

This morning I stare across the aisle at Amber as we settle into the last row seats in homeroom. Mrs. Langley raps a ruler on the desk to get our attention. "Remember, class, today is the day for parent-teacher conference meetings. You will have your first three classes at your normal schedule, and then all students are to return to homeroom and wait for your parents."

Ugh. I'm probably the only one whose parents won't show. Again.

Amber has her books pressed to her chest with her arms wrapped around them as we all stand up to leave for first period class. She grins as she glances at me sideways and she files out with the others. I admire her from the back and think again about our encounter.

Mrs. Langley interrupts my enjoyment. "Mr. Pierce, a moment please?"

That's never good. I trudge to the front of her desk and stand without a word.

"Danny," she starts, "I don't have a parent conference time scheduled with either of your parents. Did you take the flyer home to them?"

I envision the blue piece of paper still sitting on the kitchen counter along with the unopened mail. "Yes, ma'am, I took it home. I told my mama about it. My dad is gone. I don't know what else to tell you." Neither of my parents had ever once come to a meeting requested by the school. No one was going to tell them what to do.

Mrs. Langley breathes deeply as she tucks her hair behind her ear. "Okay, well if you have time between classes and have any way to reach them, maybe on the payphone in the lobby, please let them know I'm keeping the last time slot open for them. It starts at 4:15." She doesn't sound hopeful, but at least this time she doesn't seem to be blaming me.

"Yes, ma'am," I answer, heading out to my first class. The first few times this happened, I wanted to crawl into a hole and hide. I'm used to it now. For a brief moment, I wonder if one day Curtis could come to these meetings and be a parent for me like the other kids have. Amber grabs my hand. She's been waiting for me. I blush a little, but I don't let go.

"You in trouble?" she asks.

"Oh, nah," I answer. "She was just asking about this parent conference thing. My parents don't ever come to those." I shrug.

Amber scoffs. "Man, I wish my parents wouldn't come. They *both* come. Every single time. So annoying." She stops short of her first period algebra classroom door and pulls my hand down. She whispers in my ear, "I really liked yesterday." She pulls away and heads to her seat, leaving me to race to the end of the long hallway to make it to my first class before the bell rings.

These first three classes drag on forever. My thoughts are consumed with all things Amber until that bell finally rings and we head back to homeroom. Parents are already starting to wander down the hallways. Weaving through the sea of people, I'm just about to squeeze through the door when I see Amber at the end of the hall. My smile fades at the sight of two adults walking on either side of her. The woman on the left looks just like Amber without the ear piercings and dark clothes. The tall, smiling man on the right has one arm looped into Amber's.

That man is Curtis.

Recognition mixed with horror flashes across his face as his eyes lock with mine. Amber's muffled voice says something about this being her mom and dad, but nothing registers. Everything I need to know is conveyed through Curtis's eyes.

In the mass of people, I easily slip out a side exit. I start walking, and I walk for hours. Nowhere in particular. I just walk until well past dark. When the streetlights come on, I realize that Garrison has been walking silently beside me for some time. I start to feel hungry and my legs hurt, so I make my way home in the cool evening breeze.

Stepping through the side kitchen door, I am wrapped in a thick haze of sweet, sharp smoke. I know exactly what it is, and I breathe in long and deep. Mama is sitting at the dining room table. I see a stack of cash in the center of the table, and Mama is lighting a new joint from the glowing end of a spent one. Several more are lined up on the table.

I sit down next to her. She smiles a stoned, goofy smile. "There's my boy," she says, then she takes a long drag and holds it in for a moment. Exhaling, she looks at me, her head wobbling slowly side to side. Sadness covers her face. "Curtis won't be coming around anymore," she says. She points to the cash. "But he left this to help out."

Sitting back in silence, I stare into space. Mama takes another drag, then passes the joint to me. "Wanna join me?"

From this day forward through my seventeenth birthday, I am stoned every single day.

9

AGE FOURTEEN

"Where's that two-hundred-dollar receipt, Leona?! I'm about to go get my money back for this sorry excuse of a son!"

Dad stormed up the stairs to their bedroom like he always did whenever he'd threaten to unadopt me and send me back into the foster system. He had only been back in the house for three weeks, and already things were blowing up. This time though, the threat had no power.

I hate you so much! I wish you were dead!

A little while ago, Mama and I had come home early from the free clinic. She was supposed to get a prescription for some new medicine to help fix the infection on her hand that wouldn't heal right. Normally going to the clinic would take hours because of so many people. But when Mama signed in, they told her they couldn't write any more prescriptions since the actual doctor had left for an emergency. There was no point in wasting the day there, so she got some kind of cream at the drug store and we headed back home.

Mama and I had argued the whole way home.

"Why do you keep letting Dad come back in the house, Mama? All he does is sit around and smoke and make a huge mess, and he gets mad at everything and then we both get hit. Why can't you divorce him? You don't take crap from anybody, but you let him wipe his boots all over you like a doormat!"

She stared at me for a few seconds. "You're just a kid. You don't understand anything, Danny."

I threw my hands into the air. "Well, then explain it to me, Mama! He doesn't love you. He's not a husband or a dad; he never has been. You don't ever stick up for yourself. All you ever do is fight, and then he takes off for months, and then he shows back up again. And you act like nothing's wrong! What else is there to understand?!" I said a few curse words under my breath and stared out the window.

"It's not always like that!" she argued. "There's been plenty of times you haven't seen where he's treated me real good. He takes care of some things for me that you know nothing about, because you're fourteen. You're too young to know those things. Everything's not always how you think it is, Danny."

"But then why were you dating that Curtis guy?"

An odd mixture of grief and rage crossed her face. "Don't you EVER bring that up again, do you hear me?! That is none of your business, boy!"

She lit up a new cigarette and took several deep drags. After riding in silence for a few minutes, Mama said, "Love isn't always what you think it is, Danny."

I snorted. "Well, if all of this crap is what love is, then I don't want any part of it."

Something felt weird as soon as we walked in the door at home. Normally Dad would have had his feet up in the recliner watching television and smoking. That's what he normally did all day long. But the television was off, and an open bottle of vodka sat on the kitchen table. It hadn't been there when Mama and I left.

There were two empty glasses on the table next to the vodka, and a long-sleeved pink shirt that was way too small to fit Mama lay draped across the back of the kitchen chair.

Mama stared at the table for a few seconds, and then we both heard sounds coming from upstairs.

Dad was up there with a girl.

Instantly raging, Mama stormed up toward her room.

"Roland Pierce!" she screamed louder than I had ever heard her scream before. "Don't you dare tell me there's another woman up there in my bedroom! I will KILL you both!"

Garrison and Kendra stepped into the room with me as I stood frozen. I was almost glad to see them.

A loud crash of Mama kicking in her bedroom door startled me. Then the fighting began. I watched as Mama dragged the screaming, half-naked girl by her blonde curls and threw her down the stairs. Mama was cursing all kinds of ways I'd never heard her curse before.

The girl tumbled down and landed at my feet, and she scrambled to the kitchen chair to put the pink shirt back on. Crying hard, she looked at me for a quick second.

I know you! You're in the upper class at my school! You drive the rusty yellow Maverick!

I almost vomited as she ran out the front door. Then I heard a sickening crack as Mama came flying down the stairs

57

headfirst. She landed hard on her elbow, and there were bones all sticking out in weird ways.

Mama struggled to crawl away as Dad charged down the stairs, cursing up a storm.

Before I could stop myself, I stepped between him and Mama.

"Get out!" I screamed. "Now! You aren't gonna do this anymore!" The boldness in my voice surprised me.

The Bossman spoke up. "Way to go, Danny-boy! Stepping up to be the man!"

Dad's head snapped back as his eyebrows shot up. "Excuse me? Just who do you think you're talking to, boy?" He slowly inched closer and closer to me until we were almost eye to eye.

My fists clenched as I stood up to him. "You heard me! We don't want you here anymore. Mama doesn't deserve this. Get out and don't ever come back!"

A dark shadow I'd never seen before crossed my dad's face. "Boy," he growled low. "I'm gonna make you regret the day you were born."

"I already do!" I screamed in his face and braced for the beating.

"You lay a finger on him and I will have you arrested for statutory rape and attempted murder!" Mama was back up on her feet. She cradled the telephone between her shoulder and her ear as she hugged her grossly broken arm to her chest. Another voice called out "Hello" on the line.

"Yes, hello, police?" Mama answered. "My husband is attacking me inside my own house, and he just broke my arm and he won't leave. He's threatening to hurt my son. I'm afraid someone's gonna die if you don't get over here right now!"

Dad spun around and ran back up the stairs, bellowing about finding the receipt from when he bought me so he could return me to foster care.

Right now, anywhere is better than this.

Stomping around upstairs as he threw his things together to leave, Dad continued to curse and yell and threaten. I took the phone from Mama as her pain started to get worse. She collapsed in the kitchen chair just as I heard sirens coming. The cops pounded on the door a few seconds later.

I opened the door and jumped back, and three officers with guns drawn pushed through.

"Upstairs," Mama said, pained exhaustion weakening her voice. One of the officers holstered his gun and came to stand by Mama. He pulled out a walkie talkie and pressed the key.

"Officer Bellamy at 211 Ninth Street; I need an ambulance. Adult female victim has what looks like a compound fracture."

An operator on the other end of the radio squawked something back. "10-4," answered Bellamy. "Ma'am," he said as he sat next to her. "Can you tell me how this happened?"

"My dad did it," I said. "I watched him throw her down the stairs after Mama ran off the girl he had up in his bed. Mama hit her elbow real hard on the floor right there where she landed, and then her arm was all bent up. He came down after her again, but I got between them. Then he threatened to hurt me." Tears tried to erupt. I wouldn't let them.

Officer Bellamy took some notes on a small notepad. "That true, ma'am?" he asked.

Her shoulders slumped, Mama nodded. "Roland Floyd

Pierce did this to me," she moaned, her voice barely above a whisper. "He's beat me more times than I can count."

Lots of shouting and scuffling came from upstairs. A few seconds later, the officers marched my dad down the stairs, hands cuffed behind his back as he continued to curse. Catching my eye as I stood next to Mama, Dad lunged in my direction before the officers could stop him.

The last thing I remember was Brody, the Other who fights, rushing into the room as Roland Pierce spat directly in my face. Brody's swinging fist shot toward Roland's nose as I drifted away into dark numbness.

10

AGE FOURTEEN

I am fourteen, and I'm in the juvenile detention center again for something I don't remember doing. But now I want to commit murder.

With my ankles crossed, I slouch backward on the wide cement stairs that lead down to the pathetic exercise yard inside the Lexington Juvenile Detention Center. It's November, so the weather is turning cold and gusty. I pull the collar of my JDC-issued sweatshirt up to cover my ears as the icy wind whips my hair. Vapor swirls from my mouth and nose as I force myself to breathe slow and deep.

Even the name of this place is a joke. The only "services" they offer are mystery-meat dinners, lumpy mattresses, and cold floors. Dr. Scanlon, the shrink, is around if you act like a wacko, but he just sends you to solitary on pills. There's no help here. Just bars and locks.

Sometimes it still beats being home, though. The last five times I was sent here for some mess-up, it was almost a kind of relief—a break from the hell that is my life, even if it came with locked doors and rules I hated.

This time around, I'm here because I tried to beat up my dad. I don't remember most of it though. Last I can picture, Dad had just thrown my mama down the stairs in front of me. Her arm was all mangled. The cops came, for once, and they marched him out in handcuffs.

Then he spat in my face, and the room went red before Brody took over. I woke up in the back seat of the cop car, my knuckles bloody and swollen. My left pinky finger looked broken. Cops say Roland was knocked clean out. Can't say I'm not satisfied.

Thankfully I've got a couple of buddies on the inside. TJ has been here the longest, going on his fifth year. He's a gang banger, tattoos and all. When he was twelve, he got into a fight with a kid from another gang and left that kid paralyzed. TJ had already been running the streets for a couple of years, so the JDC has no idea what to do with him other than keep him locked up. He never forgets anything, and he always takes care of payback even if it's years later. He likes me though, so we're cool.

Charlie is my other buddy. We knew the same kids growing up, and we like the same kinds of music and games and stuff. I think he might have some of his own Others. I can be myself around him, so I'm glad he's my bunkmate.

This morning a new kid named Isaac showed up at breakfast. He must be at least twelve years old because all of the younger kids are in a different building. But he looks eight, maybe nine years old, tops. Scrawny and ugly, he's afraid of his own shadow. He wouldn't talk to anyone during breakfast. He just pushed his cold scrambled eggs around on his plate. A few times I saw him wiping his eyes. Every time someone would make a loud sound or scrape their chair across the floor, Isaac would jump out of his skin.

I thought about making him my punk. Then I saw the marks inside his left arm.

Three cigarette burn circles in the shape of a triangle.

Sliding my food tray over to Charlie, I stood and made my way to the seat across from Isaac.

"Hey," I said. "My name's Danny. You're Isaac, right? They told us you were coming."

Shrinking into himself, he looked at the floor and nodded.

"I'm in for beating up my dad because he hurt my mom. What are you in for?"

His voice was so soft I could barely understand his answer. "Running away."

"Yeah, I've been there, man. What'd you run away for?"

He pulled down the sleeves of his oversized JDC-issued sweatshirt and crossed his arms. "None of your business."

I raised my palms. "Okay, man, no problem."

We sat in awkward silence for a while. I cleared my throat. "Okay, well, over there at the middle table, the big dude with the frizzy hair, that's TJ. He's a gang banger, so whatever you do, don't get on his bad side. He'll leave you alone otherwise. Across from him with the blond choirboy hair is Charlie. He's nice. If you see him talking to himself, just leave him alone. That boy in the corner that looks like a linebacker is Nicky. Everybody stays as far away from him as possible. Watch out for Officer Pelham, he's the one with the massive beer belly and the pizza face. He hates being here and hates kids even more. Officer Dunkirk is cool, it seems like he cares about us, you know?"

"Why are you being nice to me?"

I pulled up my own sleeve and laid my arm on the table. At the recognition of my scars, Isaac drew his own arms closer into himself. He wiped an escaping tear with his shoulder.

I pushed my sleeve down again. "I remember what it was like on my first day in JDC. Plus a lot of us in here have been through the same crap storm. Sometimes it's nice to know you're not the only one. I know it's helped me."

Standing up to leave, I heard a quiet "Thanks" and stuck out my hand. Isaac studied me for a few seconds, then he finally accepted my handshake.

"Nice to meet you, Isaac. See ya 'round."

As soon as Charlie and I got back to our pod after breakfast, Officer Dunkirk stood next to my bed with a trash bag. "New bunkmate, boys," he said, tossing the bag up to the top bunk. "Keep him away from Nicky, would ya?" he asked as Isaac came up behind us escorted by Officer Pelham.

"This is where little boys who run away from home get to live," said Pizza-face with a sneer. "Breaking the rules will get you a trip to solitary. Got it?"

Isaac's shoulders relaxed when he saw me and Charlie. "Yes, sir," he squeaked. Climbing up onto his bunk, he untied his trash bag and pulled out the sad little pile of his things. He quickly shoved a small, brown teddy bear under his pillow and wiped away another tear.

"Yo, Isaac, me and Charlie were gonna head out to the exercise yard if you wanna come," I offered.

Considering his options for a moment, Isaac nodded and jumped down from his bunk.

Once we were all outside, Charlie headed straight for the

basketball court. Isaac and I made our way to the far corner of the wide cement stairs that led down to the yard. This part of the stairs was still in the sun, and we could lean back against a fence railing and watch the whole yard.

We sat in total silence for a good thirty minutes. Isaac had stopped crying, and he watched the group of boys in the exercise yard with a mixture of curiosity and distrust.

He eventually broke the silence. "What happened to you?" he asked, tipping his head toward my arm.

I stretched out my still-swollen hand. "I blacked out and punched my dad in the face until he was unconscious. Think my pinky is broken." I winced as I opened and closed my fist.

"No, I mean your arm. The scars," he answered, staring at the ground.

"Oh, that," I said. "Let's just say that I used to live with some sick, evil people."

"Evil," Isaac echoed. "That's a good word for it. Definitely evil."

Isaac toyed with a small ant near his foot before smashing it with his toe. "You had them scars long?" he asked.

I looked up at the sky as I did the math in my head. "I don't know, maybe eight or ten years? Something like that. I was in foster care, so it was before I got adopted. You?"

"About two years ago, I guess. That was when I ran away the first time."

We watched the terribly one-sided basketball game for a few plays. It's a miracle that no one was throwing punches.

"Come on, Charlie!" I yelled. "Gotta be quicker on that rebound!"

Sticking out his tongue and saluting me with his middle finger, Charlie grinned and charged back into the game.

"You said you got adopted?" Isaac asked, picking at a hangnail on his thumb.

"Yeah, I think I was about eight. Wasn't a whole lot better than foster care. I mean, some of it was better." I opened and closed my sore hands again. "Obviously it wasn't great."

Picking up a lone piece of pine straw from the ground and tossing it into the wind, Isaac turned toward me. "Anybody ever help you? Like, anybody ever get in trouble for what they did to you?" The sadness in his face and the dark circles under his eyes hurt my heart.

I cursed. "Definitely not. Two days ago was the first time the cops ever came to help my mom, and I've been there," I paused to do the math. "What's fourteen minus eight?"

"Six."

"I've been there six years, and not one police officer, not one child services worker, not one single school counselor or teacher has ever once lifted a finger to help me."

Glancing at the basketball game again, I shot up to my feet. "Charlie, watch the screen!" I slapped my forehead as Charlie took a hard elbow to the chin. After a few shoves and shouting, they resumed the game.

Sitting down, I massaged the knuckles around my broken finger. "What about you?" I asked, wincing at the pain. "Anybody ever help you?"

Isaac thought for a moment. "Nah. I mean, there was this one lady at the county office who seemed super nice. I don't remember her name, but she was older with long white hair that she kept in a braid. I told her about some of the stuff that was going on in my foster home, the one I've been at for four years now. She was actually sad for me and said she'd help me. Next thing I know, somebody gave my case file to

66

someone else. The new child services lady told my foster parents that I was a pathological liar and that I probably needed mental treatment. Then I never saw another child services person again. That's been about a year now. And they wonder why I keep running away."

The next month went by fast. Other than talking with me and Charlie, Isaac kept to himself. He spent most of his time reading books. Some nights he would wake us up as he fought off an evil abuser in his dreams. I would never tell Isaac the nasty things he would talk about in his sleep, mostly because they sounded too close to home.

This morning, Isaac's sentence at JDC ended. He'd gained a little weight from eating three times a day, which apparently wasn't a normal thing for him at home. After we shook hands, I made my way outside to the back corner of the cement stairs above the exercise yard. The bars of the fence railing gave a somewhat unobstructed view of the drop-off and pickup zone in front of the JDC building.

A rusted old blue Chevy Impala was parked at the end of the sidewalk. Its motor running, the car's oily exhaust rose from the tailpipe like a mist in the cold. A stocky young man wearing a Yankees baseball cap held Isaac's arm firmly as they hustled to the car. Opening the back door, the man shoved Isaac into the back seat and kicked the door shut.

White-hot rage began to swirl from deep inside as I watched the hefty man remove his Yankees hat and run his fingers through his thick, red hair.

I will murder Carl Blackwell with my bare hands if it's the last thing I ever do.

11

AGE EIGHTEEN

I am eighteen years old, and I am crazy.

Crazy for Jesus.

I sit in this huge church between Dean and Linda Baxter, and I look around the room in grateful wonder.

I still cannot believe I love this so much.

Garrison does NOT like being in this church. He prefers to stay outside. Kendra still hangs in the back corner, but she stays busy writing the biblical instructions coming from the pulpit so she can use it as ammunition against me later.

As the worship music starts, my thoughts travel back to the first time I was dragged into this place a year ago.

"You have the potential to be the most successful thief in The Pit," Uncle Mickey had said.

Taking me under his wing, Uncle Mickey had seen how easily breaking and entering came to me. I could be in and out of a house with loot in six minutes flat. Uncle Mickey was so impressed that he started assigning me solo jobs. My cut of the take was pretty sweet—it kept gas in my Chevy Vega and dope in my pocket.

Last July, Uncle Mickey had pulled me next to him as he flipped hot dogs on the grill in his cousin's back yard. He looked around, then bent his head close to mine. "Got a job for you, boy. Needs to be tomorrow at noon. High stakes."

The smoky, sizzling hot dogs made my mouth water. "Fourth of July?" I asked. "Ain't that kinda risky? I mean I'm game, but…"

"Yep, noon tomorrow." He took a long swig of his Budweiser. "Family's out of town. Packed up their station wagon and took off early this morning. Supposed to be gone through Monday."

I scratched at the thin beard I was trying to grow. "Cool, cool," I said. "Where's the job?"

Uncle Mickey looked around again before he answered. "It's that Jesus church guy over on the corner of Lanning and First in Rucker Hills."

My hand covered my mouth and my eyebrows shot up. "Yeah! No way, man! That's so cool!" I was louder than I should have been.

Motioning his hand to shush me, he glared at me. "Easy, boy. Yeah it's high stakes, but it's just another job."

At noon the next day, I slipped a stolen credit card into the door jamb. The years of experience with breaking and entering served me well my fingers felt the resistance to the latch. In only a few seconds, the door opened easily without a sound. Holding my breath, I listened for anything that may have given me away. Satisfying silence welcomed me, and I slipped inside.

I had been looking forward to getting into this particular

house for months. The clueless homeowner, the round-bellied guy with the giant bald spot and the ridiculous "Jesus Loves You" sticker on the bumper of his wood-paneled station wagon, had no clue about my casing this place. He even smiled and waved at me once as our cars passed on the street.

Noon on the Fourth of July was a perfect time to hit this place. No one would expect a robbery in broad daylight on a holiday. I checked my watch. One minute after noon.

I bounded up the stairs two at a time and pushed every door open until I found the master.

Jackpot!

A tall wooden jewelry box on top of the dresser caught my eye. I opened it quickly and dumped the sparkly contents into the massive pocket inside my trench coat. Then I tossed the empty jewelry box over my shoulder and let it crash. Trashing every dresser drawer, I came away with several nice watches, a small camera, and a book of bank checks. Kendra was in the corner, recording my every move. I didn't care.

Uncle Mickey's gonna love this.

I headed to the closet next and scored a nice .38 Special on the top shelf. A rifle was stored in the corner of the closet, but it was too long to risk. Then a small safe on the floor caught my eye. As I knelt to investigate the lock, I froze.

Voices echoed up the stairs.

Before I had time to react, the Jesus church guy and his frizzy-headed wife walked into the room. Their conversation stopped midsentence.

The woman gasped at the mess as the Jesus guy spotted me.

"Honey," he said. "Get downstairs right now and call the

police to report that we've walked in on a robbery. Tell them to send help quickly."

Hand flying to her mouth, she rushed out the door. I went to grab the handgun I'd just dumped into my coat pocket, but the homeowner grabbed my arm before I could get to it. Up close I realized how tall he actually was.

"What do you think you're doing, son?" he asked. His lack of rage caught me off guard. I tried to fish for the gun again, but this man was much faster and stronger. He pulled the .38 from my pocket before I could blink, and dumping the bullets, he held the gun down to his side.

"How old are you, son? Fifteen? Sixteen?"

"Seventeen," I answered, my voice cracking. I tried to wriggle out of his grip, but he easily outweighed me by twice.

"Ah-ah-ah," he scolded. "You know I can't just let you leave, right? You've broken the law, son."

The woman called up the stairs. "They're on their way, Dean!"

The man looked at me with surprising kindness. "So, obviously the police are on their way." Gun still in his hand, he stepped back to the bedroom door and closed it. "May as well have a seat, son."

"I ain't your son," I snapped.

"You're somebody's son," he answered.

My chin jutted and eyes narrowed in angry defiance, I snorted. "You don't know nothin'."

The guy stood there like Garrison often did, feet apart and arms crossed as he boomed. "SIT. DOWN. NOW."

My shoulders slumped as I plopped down onto a small wooden chair in the corner. Garrison and Brody came into the room and stood next to Kendra.

Jesus church guy moved to sit on the edge of the bed right in front of me. He still held the gun, but it wasn't pointed at me. "My name is Dean Baxter. What's your name, kid?"

I looked out the window. "I ain't gotta tell you nothin'."

"Well, I'm Dean. My wife's name is Linda. We have three boys. Benjamin just turned twenty-five. He's getting married next month. Peter is twenty-one, and he's up at Ohio State playing the trumpet in the marching band. And Mark is eighteen, he's graduating this year and he plans to join the Air Force. If you're from around here you might even be at the same school. There's his senior picture on the wall right there. Maybe you recognize him?"

Something snapped. "I'm not looking at your STUPID son's picture! I don't need to hear about your perfect life, church man. Whose son am I? I ain't nobody's son. My real mama was a crazy drug addict prostitute, and the only daddies I've ever had were evil psychos. You sit there looking all rich and perfect. You ain't got a clue, man." I added a few choice curse words to make my point.

Dean looked me in the eye with patient kindness. "I'm truly sorry to hear what you've been through. I'm sure it must have been really tough."

Nobody had ever said they were sorry for me.

"Careful, Danny," said the Bossman. "Get a grip."

"Have you ever been arrested before?" asked Dean. It wasn't accusing. It was curious.

"Plenty," I said, my eyes on the floor.

"Can you look at me for a moment, son?"

I couldn't not look up at the tenderness of his voice. I was met with unexpected eyes of love.

"I want you to know that I forgive you."

An unexpected tsunami of guilt and shame slammed into me. Four-year-old Tiny Tot, one of the Others, peeked around from behind Kendra. He's the only one who is allowed to cry. I pinched the bridge of my nose to push back the tears and I waved Tiny Tot away.

The wail of a police siren hit my ears. Glancing out the window, I saw a patrol car as it squealed into the driveway. Two cops jumped out of the car, guns raised. I covered my eyes with my hand. "Oh, man," I groaned.

Kendra wrote furiously as she stood next to Brody and Tiny Tot.

Keeping an eye on me, Dean stood up and opened the door. "Up here, officers," he called, slipping the gun into his pocket.

I was already down on my knees by the time they stormed into the room. "On the ground NOW!" the first cop screamed. The second cop dug a knee into my back as he handcuffed me from behind. Then he roughly pulled me up onto my feet as the first cop put his gun away.

"Well, lookie who we have here, Walt. If it isn't Danny Pierce, our favorite punk!" he said with a smirk.

Cop Walt snorted. "Of course it's you. Man, Travis, this must be our lucky day! Danny, Judge Mossberg is gonna put you away until you forget your own name."

Dean held his hand up. "Officer, I believe he's still got some of our possessions there in his coat pocket. Would it be okay if I retrieve those things?"

Item by item, Cop Travis pulled every bit of loot from the pocket in my coat and set it all out on the bed. Cop Walt flipped open a small notepad and started writing a list of everything I'd stolen. Disappointment grew as I calculated the cash value of the loot in my head.

Then a thought punched me in the gut.

Uncle Mickey is gonna murder me!

Catching Dean's eye, I could tell he had seen the wave of horror cross my face. I looked away, my cheeks flushed.

Sure that my pockets were empty, Cop Travis grabbed my shoulder to walk me out. Dean cleared his throat as he followed close behind. "Officers, could you tell me what's likely to happen with this young man?"

"Well, we're kinda sick of running into this kid," Cop Walt answered as we made our way down the stairs. "Judge Mossberg has warned him over and over, but clearly it never got through his thick skull. He's probably looking at twenty-five years for being a habitual offender."

Twenty-five years… I'll be an old man!

Cop Travis recited the familiar phrase as we made our way to the door. "Danny Pierce, you are under arrest for robbery and for breaking and entering. You have the right to remain silent. Anything you say can and will be used against you in a court of law. You have the right to an attorney…"

The cop's voice faded to a dull buzz. A crying Tiny Tot scrambled to join me as I was lowered into the back of the police car. Certain my life was over, I closed my tear-filled eyes to escape beneath the surface.

Three days later, I was escorted into a courtroom for my arraignment. Wearing an orange prison jumpsuit and shackled by the hands and feet, several other detainees along with me shuffled in front of Judge Mossberg's bench.

Public Defender Harris, a sloppy little man with an ever-runny nose, read each of our charges aloud. Despite the heaviness connected to all of our charges, the guy read them with the interest and passion of a history teacher on the last day of school. Kendra stood close by, her glare boring into my soul, as Brody paced along the back wall.

My case was the last to be heard. I stood but I could only stare at the floor as fear and shame swirled in my gut. My face reddened at the idea that Uncle Mickey should've been in there with me. He dragged me into this mess in the first place.

Defender Harris flipped through multiple folders, finally finding my case page. "Good morning, Your Honor. My client is present with counsel, and we are requesting bail until such time as counsel can arrange conference."

A man's voice spoke loudly from the seating area behind me. "Your Honor, may I make a statement to this court as the victim of Danny Pierce's recent actions?"

Everyone in the courtroom turned toward the speaker. My jaw dropped.

It was the Jesus church guy Dean Baxter.

Judge Mossberg sat up and looked over his reading glasses. "Make it quick, sir."

Dean Baxter stepped out from his seat and walked up to the wooden partition gate that separated the criminals and attorneys from the observing public. "Your Honor, my name is Dean Baxter. I understand just a little of the history of this young man. Is it true that he broke into my house to rob me? Yes, it is. I walked in and caught him red-handed, so according to the laws of the state of Kentucky, he actually deserves every punishment this court wants to inflict. But Your Honor, I'm a follower of Jesus Christ. I'm a Christian, and I'm one of the associate pastors at Bethel Fellowship church in Rucker Hills. And I feel compelled first of all to drop all of the charges against this young man as an act of forgiveness."

The few people in the room all gasped.

Dean Baxter continued. "Furthermore, Your Honor, I would like to make a proposal to this court. Surely you recognize the cost that the state of Kentucky would incur by putting this kid away for years as he deserves. I would like to offer an alternative solution. If it please the court, I would like to request temporary guardianship over Mr. Pierce until his eighteenth birthday. I would further request that the court order Mr. Pierce to attend Sunday church services at Bethel Fellowship with me every single Sunday for the next year as his sentence. And should he fail to comply with this condition of weekly church attendance, Mr. Pierce would immediately forfeit his freedom and be returned to the custody of the state."

Church every single Sunday? UGH. County jail might be better than that.

Removing his glasses, Judge Mossberg leaned forward and propped his elbows on his desk. "This is a highly unusual request, Mr. Baxter. I have to tell you, this young man has been in this courtroom more times than I can count, and every case is worse than the last. I'm not sure that you fully understand the kind of young man he truly is."

Dean Baxter lowered his head, took a deep breath, and looked back up with a soft smile. "Your Honor, I actually see some of myself in this young man. I believe that Mr. Pierce may be the victim of neglect and poor parenting, and I'd be willing to bet that no one has ever actually given him a chance in a healthy environment. Somebody gave me a chance when

I was his age, and it completely changed everything about my life."

Tiny Tot stepped out from behind Kendra. I hung my head and squeezed my eyes shut.

I'm NOT gonna cry. Go away, Tiny Tot!

The courtroom was dead quiet for several long moments. Tapping his desk with a finger as he stared at the ceiling, Judge Mossberg took a long, deep breath. Then he looked at me.

"Mr. Pierce, do you understand what's being offered here today?"

I shrugged. "I dunno, I mean, I guess so. Not sure how I feel about it, though. Sounds kinda stupid."

"Mr. Pierce, are you aware that, because of your past record, you're now looking at some serious state prison time? You've worn out your welcome at the county lockup, and you're too old for JDC. You'd be on the inside of the Kentucky State Penitentiary with some of the most hardened felons east of the Mississippi. Does that sound like a better option, son?"

One of Uncle Mickey's boys got shanked there last month.

My mouth dry and my heart racing, I dropped my head. "No, Your Honor."

"Look up here, Mr. Pierce."

I wondered if I might fit under the desk to crawl away from the seriousness of the judge's expression.

"Normally when I have a kid like you come through my courtroom, Mr. Pierce, I find myself actually looking forward to throwing the whole book at you. You've stood here time and again and listened to me give you warning after warning about the direction your life is heading. It goes in one ear and out the other. So, hear me clearly, Mr. Pierce. You deserve nothing less than a career stay at the state penitentiary."

Judge Mossberg paused to look at Dean Baxter.

"Now," he continued, "this churchgoing man, whom I've never met before, apparently sees something in you that none of the rest of us can see, including yourself. Not only has he decided not to press charges against you for the crimes that you clearly committed, this man is offering to take you into an environment of stability and accountability at his own expense, with absolutely no guarantee that he can trust you."

His words hung heavy in the room as a new wave of shame washed through me.

"Mr. Baxter, are you willing to put up a security bond in the event that Mr. Pierce fails to comply with this order and then goes AWOL?"

Dean Baxter didn't hesitate. "Yes, Your Honor, I am."

Why would a stranger do this for me?

"Any objections, counsel?"

Leaning in close, the public defender placed an arm over my shoulder as he whispered, "You're an idiot if you don't take this offer, kid." I nodded. "No objections, Your Honor. My client accepts the stipulations."

Two weeks later, I walked into Bethel Fellowship Church with Dean and Linda Baxter. That day, I heard for the very first time that there was a real God in heaven who loved me, and that His perfect Son allowed Himself to be murdered so that I could be rescued.

It took several more months of fatherly love from Dean Baxter, and lots of patient question-and-answer sessions with Linda, for me to come to the truth about Jesus. Six months after walking into that church, responding to the invitation to accept God's priceless gift of salvation, and making it public by getting baptized in front of everyone, was the greatest day of my life.

And now I think I've finally figured out why the Others are here. This battle in my mind has to be what the pastor calls spiritual warfare. It all finally makes sense.

Clapping me on the back this morning at church, Dean Baxter beams at me with pride. A small tear of gratitude forms as I take in the words of the hymn sung by the choir.

I stand amazed in the presence
Of Jesus the Nazarene,
And wonder how He could love me,
A sinner condemned, unclean.

He took my sins and my sorrows,
He made them His very own;
He bore the burden to Calvary,
And suffered, and died alone.

How marvelous! How wonderful!
And my song shall ever be:
How marvelous! How wonderful!
Is my Savior's love for me!

Hard to believe just how much Jesus loves me.

12

AGE FORTY-EIGHT

The underfed teenage girl in front of me chews her dirty fingernails as her foot bounces. The dark circles under her eyes and the scars on her forearms spark brief images of my own similar wounds. Anger flashes at the sight of the three small cigarette burn circles in a triangle on her arm. I swallow the thoughts down with my coffee.

A career as a high school counselor was never even remotely on my radar. But after Grace and I married and started having kids of our own, I began to grow more painfully aware of just how many people had failed me as a child. Then some friends we met at church happened to be guidance counselors in the public school system. They had a genuine interest in helping troubled students, and the more I interacted with them, the more I saw the calling on their lives to make a real difference. It became my calling. Now, every single day, I'm rewarded with the gift of listening to a broken kid's story the way no one ever did for me. I could live without the ridiculous administrative demands. But it's usually worth it.

Many days I leave work grieved for a student who's in a real mess. My own children, Josiah and Abigail, have no idea just how much they ease that burden for me. Every night as I tuck them into bed and pray God's protection over them, I remind myself of the vows I made when they were born, to protect them like I wasn't protected. My craziness and my ongoing battle with the Others hasn't been easy on them, and I know sometimes I make our lives hard. I pray often that God shields their hearts from my failures.

Today, fifteen-year-old Aimee Dixon watches me with guarded curiosity as I flip through the pages of her Individual Educational Plan. Marched into my office by the exasperated Creative Arts teacher after a scuffle with a fellow student, Aimee oozes rebellion from her narrowed eyes. The cluster of neon purple hair at her bangs accentuate her defiance.

Noticing very little documentation in her file about her home life, I lean back. "So, Miss Dixon, I'd love to hear your side of the story. Can you tell me what happened?"

Her eyes roll as she crosses her arms. She considers me for a moment before answering.

"Art is the one class I'm good at, Mr. Pierce. And that spoiled brat Olivia has to make everybody else feel like crap about their work so she can feel better about hers. Which sucks by the way. I got tired of Mrs. Strobel looking the other way, so I got in Olivia's face. Nobody ever stands up to the bullies around here."

A pang of guilt in my gut confirms the sad truth of her statement.

"Well, Miss Dixon," I begin.

"Don't call me that. My name's Aimee. Dixon isn't my real last name. My birth mom's last name was Joyner."

So many similarities.

"All right, Aimee. Some of your other teachers tell me there's more going on than just what happened in art class today. Your homeroom teacher is noticing that you've been falling asleep before first period even starts. Mr. Everhart says you've missed most of your homework assignments for the last couple of months, but before that you had a decent grade in his class. You've been to the nurse's office more times in the last several weeks than you have since you started here at Kingston."

"Yeah, so?" she snaps. "It ain't a crime to be sick."

"No one is saying that, Miss Dix... Aimee. But several people who have spent some time with you can tell that something is up."

Turning her head to stare out the window where red and orange leaves float by, Aimee bites her lip. She starts to answer and stops herself, wrestling with her emotions.

I sit back. "Aimee, I understand that you don't want to air your dirty laundry with the school counselor. You're free not to tell me anything at all. But I do want you to know that I think I understand some of what you're going through."

Still staring out the window and closing her eyes, she drops her head, "You don't know anything."

I roll up my left shirt sleeve and rest my arm toward her on the desk. "I want to show you something."

Her eyes grow wide as she sees the remnants of old cigarette burns on my forearm. Three burn circles in a triangle. Cheeks flushing and shoulders slumped, she turns away again and reaches to hide her own scars from view.

I roll my sleeve down and fasten the button at the cuff. "Pierce isn't my real last name either. I'm actually not even sure what my real last name was supposed to have been. Some truly awful people adopted me so I got stuck with it."

Aimee turns slowly to face me, mouth slightly agape, eyes softening a bit.

"Now before we go any further," I continue, "I need to clarify a few things about our conversation. As a counselor, everything you and I discuss is confidential for the most part. But there are a couple of very specific exceptions. First, if I believe that you are in serious danger of harming yourself or bringing serious harm to another person, I'm required by law to report that. Also, if you disclose to me that there's a minor child currently being harmed by someone, including harm being done to you, that kind of thing also has to be reported. I cannot promise any confidentiality with these things. Do you have any questions about what I just said?"

She shakes her head no.

Grabbing a pencil and my legal pad, I turn back to her IEP. "So there isn't a ton of information in your file about your family situation. Would you mind just telling me a little bit of your story? Doesn't have to be detailed unless you want it to be. But I am especially interested in what's been going on the last few months, if you want to share."

Drawing her knees up to her chin, Aimee wraps her thin arms around her legs and rests her head on one knee. She takes a long breath and closes her eyes. "Birth mom was an addict. Died when I was born. My real dad was in jail. Never met him. Straight into foster care. The first couple of homes were okay. In third grade those people adopted me. But a couple years later they got a divorce, and she started drinking and he went psycho. He tried to burn the house down with us inside. So back into foster care I went."

My heart hurts as I write her story.

She's quiet for a few moments. "The next foster home was like heaven," she continues, softer. "The foster mom, Lucy, she was like a real mom, you know? She'd make food that I liked to eat, she'd sit and help me with my homework. She bought me my first set of acrylics. She's the one who got me started with painting. There was nobody like her."

She wipes a lone tear with the heel of her hand and shakes her head with a sniff. "But around my thirteenth birthday, I guess some rules with the system changed about how big a foster home has to be, or some other stupid rule like that. So one day this short, fat lady knocked on the door and told Lucy that her license had been revoked. Took me straight to another foster home. Sickest old redheaded pervert you've ever seen. I've been living in hell ever since. Well, up until two months ago, since I ran away."

A slight wave of nausea rolls through my gut. "What do you mean by sickest old pervert?"

"Doesn't matter," she says flatly.

Laying down my pen, I fold my hands under my chin. "Aimee, is someone hurting you?"

"I'm not saying that. But even if I were, it wouldn't matter. I'd be blamed and then nothing would happen."

I write in silence and I wait.

Shifting in her chair, Aimee folds her legs under herself. "So anyway, I started dating this guy, Simon, over the summer. He's seen some stuff too, you know. He tells me how he had filed a petition to become an emancipated minor when he was sixteen so he could get out of a rough situation. He got approved and got his GED and enrolled himself in the Vo-Tech school to get certified as a mechanic. I looked into the emancipation thing, and so I'm doing all the things I have to do so I can file."

"What kinds of things?"

"A job was the biggest issue. Not a lot of places want to hire a fifteen-year-old, but Simon's cousin Layla is the manager over at Nell's Diner, so she's letting me work there. I had to run away from the foster home I was at. That sorry excuse of a human who calls himself my foster father wouldn't let me work or paint or anything. He even sent me to juvie. Once he claimed I was stealing from him when I took food from the pantry when he was gone. Another time I actually found him with my wallet, and all my cash inside was gone. I took it back while he was asleep, so he charged me with theft and sent me back to juvie. So I left, and now I'm living with Simon and Layla and her mom Louise."

I raise an eyebrow.

Aimee's cheeks flush. "It's not like that. I'm not stupid. We're not having sex. We're not doing drugs. I sleep on the couch and Simon has his own room. Louise don't play."

"Good."

A quick thought zips through my mind that she might need to turn to God, but I dismiss the idea as fast as it comes.

Whole lot of good God has done for me the last thirty years.

I haven't doubted the gift of salvation that Jesus gave me as a teenager. But the constant struggle for my sanity has taken its toll over the decades. No sense giving Aimee any more emotional conflict. Better to keep that to myself.

"I was able to talk to the same legal aid rep that Simon

used," she continues. "That guy said because the foster home I ran away from has a history of complaints and because I've started the emancipation paperwork, nobody can come after me and force me to go back. He's getting me a guardian ad litem until it's all filed. He also said there could actually be some kind of criminal case in the works, and I might even be able to testify if it comes to that. I don't know about that, but I'm just happy to be out of that god-awful place."

Pride swells within me.

Oh, had I had just a fraction of her drive when I was fifteen.

"So, you're working. You're needing to keep your grades up to graduate. And you have all of this going on. It's no wonder that you're exhausted."

Tears fill her eyes as she nods.

I put down my pencil and clasp my hands. "So, what can I do to help? You already have an IEP in place. Do we want to look at some schedule adjustments? Maybe find out what alternatives are available for homework assignments?"

Her eyebrows shoot up. "You'd do that for me?" She covers her mouth to hide her surprised smile.

Tenderness flows as I sense a deep heart connection with Aimee that she probably cannot fathom. "Aimee, you may not believe me, but it's actually kinda scary how similar my story is to yours. Nobody helped me. It's an absolute miracle of the grace of God that I'm even still alive today. Because nobody would help me, that's why I decided to become a school counselor, so that I could help the ones that need help the most. So, yes. I will absolutely do that for you."

Exploding out of her chair, she darts around the desk to squeeze me tight. I fight my own tears as the bell rings.

"Give me a week to meet with your teachers, and we'll sit down and hammer out the details."

Unable to speak, she nods and wipes her eyes before she turns to leave.

"Aimee," I call after her. She stops and turns, locking eyes with me. "I'm incredibly proud of you."

After another quick hug, she dashes out the door.

God, help me to help her the way I needed help, whatever it takes.

13

AGE FORTY-EIGHT

The sight of my cluttered office desk makes me groan again. I'm not sure why I react with this much annoyance every single morning. I wish one of the Others in my head was a clean freak who took over on occasion. That'd be nice.

As I slide into the chair surrounded by student files and stacks of binders, Principal Miller's words from our early morning meeting hang with the weight of boulders on my back.

"We have some concerns," she had said. "The Towson kid played you. His violent manifesto would be all over the news if it weren't for my cleanup. That would have totally invalidated the additional funding push for this department. The superintendent and I need to make sure you're on the same page with us. Do you want me to transfer some of your more recent student cases to the trainees?"

As my boss lectured me, Kendra stood right behind her as usual, gleefully scribbling away. The Bossman chimed in several times with, "You've got this, Danny," and, "Don't let her get to you. It was one bad day. Everyone has those. You're fine."

Hoping my annoyance at her offer to pawn off my work wasn't obvious, I had said all the right things to assure Principal Miller of my capability and my commitment. I'm not sure she believed me.

Back in my office, I look around at the reports screaming for referral to child services. There's Kelly Kettering's file. She's the bewildered kid stuck in the middle of an ugly custody battle. I owe the guardian ad litem a call, but he's probably still hung over this time of the morning. I make a mental note to call him after lunch.

There's Trent Norman's file with the repetitive instances of bullying. The assistant principal from the kid's prior school owes me some records, but I think he's still angry at me for finding out that he'd covered for a teacher's inappropriate relationship. I make a mental note to have a trainee reach out.

There's the Zoe Brawner file, the crackhead kid with a crackhead mom. Ugh. It's way too early for this one. I may have done plenty of dope myself, but I wasn't stupid enough to have a kid back then. This can wait until tomorrow.

My eyes fall on the Aimee Dixon file. My heart pounds as I open the file and start flipping through the pages. Aimee reminds me so much of myself. Her story, the look in her eyes, her traumas, even her scars. So similar to mine, it's unnerving.

As I read further, I hear a familiar voice in my head. "Careful, Danny," warns the Bossman. "Don't get too immersed in this situation. It'll only lead to trouble."

"I'm helping her because nobody ever helped me," I say under my breath.

"Well, in case you forgot, you're kinda crazy," he taunts. "Digging into Aimee's life is only gonna make things worse for you. Don't be stupid, Danny-boy. How about let's go ride the Scooby Doo roller coaster like we used to?"

I clench my teeth. "I'm not riding anything with you. And I'm not stupid! I told you not to call me that!"

A human interrupts from the other side of my office. "Who... who are you talking to, Mr. Pierce?"

Jumping slightly, I'm startled to see Josh, one of the senior student trainees, standing just inside my door, brows furrowed and mouth agape.

"Uh, yes. Um, I mean, no," I stammer. I shake my head and flash a smile. "Sorry, just arguing with myself in my head. Didn't realize I was doing that out loud."

Josh considers me for a moment and slowly hands me a thick legal-sized envelope. "Principal Miller asked me to get these to you. She said these are the counselor records for Trent Norman's file."

"Well I guess the guy decided to forgive me after all," I say as I take the documents.

His eyebrows rising, Josh steps backward to make his exit. "Okay, then," he manages as he slips through my office door.

"Thanks, man!" I call after him without looking up, flipping through the pages he delivered.

A soft thought floats through my mind. "Danny, keep helping Aimee."

Dropping Trent's file, I flip to the last few pages of Aimee's documents. I recognize the school system guardianship authorization forms I've been looking for.

The purpose of this notification is to inform you that the youth below is in the temporary legal custody of Fayette County, Division of Family and Children Services/Kentucky Department of Human Services.

Child's name: Dixon, Aimee Marie.
D.O.B. April 2, 2010.
Place of birth: Lexington, KY.
Current residential status: Foster guardianship
Active Guardian ad Litem? No
Do the student's biological parents have parental rights? No
Foster care case manager: Helen Marzoni (502) 564-3440
Individualized educational plan in place? Yes
Current caregiver name(s): Carl and Melissa Blackwell

Oh. My. GOD! NO NO NO NO
This cannot be happening.
Aimee's foster parent is Carl Blackwell?!
Reeling in a mixture of confusion and rage, I calculate the math. I was eight when I moved in with the Blackwells, and Carl was seventeen. Nine years older than I am. Today I'm forty-eight, making him fifty-seven. Disgust curls the top corner of my lip.

Agonizing realization slams into my heart as I roll up my

left sleeve and trace the still-raised outline of three burn circles in a triangle. The face of a scrawny, scared little kid from JDC pops into my mind. What was his name? Isaiah? Ivan? Isaac? I-something. Remembering the same triangle of burns on his arm, I recall my rage at recognizing the stocky redheaded man who picked up the poor kid from JDC. I knew it was Carl then. It has to be the same Carl now.

I start to hyperventilate.

He was branding every one of us.

I scramble to lean over my waste can as I'm unable to stop the eruption from my stomach. After my breakfast is emptied into the trash, I flop back into my chair and cover my face with my hands.

This is too much.

The thought of running out the door until I find some oncoming traffic pops into my mind. Then I begin to hear the sound of a roller coaster track chain as it slowly pulls a string of cars up a steep wooden hill, clacking and shaking as it climbs. Tinkly park music and the aroma of popcorn and funnel cakes drift into my consciousness.

"C'mon, Danny, let's ride Scooby Doo," offers the Bossman.

Don't mind if I do.

14

AGE FORTY-EIGHT

I pinch the bridge of my nose against the sinus headache pulsing through my head and start to make a mental checklist of the things I'd need to wrap up if I were to knock off early and claim a sick day. My thoughts are interrupted by a quick knock on my door.

"Yes?" I bark, unable to hide my irritation.

Trainee Josh cracks my door open just a few inches. "Umm... Mr. Pierce, umm, there's a student in the nurse's office asking for a visit with you. Her last name is Dixon."

I'll stay for her.

I stand and nod. "Thanks, yep, she can come on to my office whenever she's ready."

"Danny, DO NOT under any circumstances tell her that you know about Carl!" orders the Bossman. "You're not even positive it's the same guy, and it would make things worse."

I don't feel like arguing today. "Understood," I answer.

Opening my top desk drawer, I fish around for the bottle of headache relief tablets with one hand as I press the "Do

Not Disturb" button on my phone with the other. Emptying the final three pills from the bottle, I toss them back with a long swig of my caffeine-charged cola. Then I close the open files strewn across my workspace, replacing them in the "to-do" pile and placing Aimee's file on the center of my desk. Taking a seat, I clasp my hands behind my head and close my eyes, willing the medicine and caffeine to work fast. After several long, deep cleansing breaths, I almost start to drift into a nap.

The soft clearing of a throat calls me awake.

"Mr. Pierce?" asks Aimee. "I'm sorry, the nurse said I could come on in. I can come back if this isn't a good time."

Stretching my arms and yawning wide, I sit forward. "No, come on in, I was just resting my brain for a second." I sniff hard and shake my head, grateful to notice less pain behind my eyes. "So what's up? How's it going? Did you have a nice holiday break?"

Noticeably less frail, Aimee sits up straight in the chair across from me. There is a healthy flush to her skin and a lightness in her eyes. The formerly purple hair at her bangs has been updated to an electric green, and she's painted her fingernails to match.

"I'm actually doing so good, Mr. Pierce. The schedule change and the homework accommodations helped way more than I thought they would. Simon's aunt Louise is super nice. I mean, like, she definitely has rules and stuff, but she doesn't treat me like I'm a stupid little kid, you know? Plus she's a pretty mean cook. She's teaching me how to make some of her best dishes. She spent all day New Year's Eve showing me how to bake homemade bread."

I nod and smile. "That's fantastic, Aimee. I'm so glad to hear that."

"She actually read about this art competition at a gallery over in the Little Five Points art district, and she's super excited for me to enter. There's a bunch of contest stages, and it'll take a while. But the grand prize winner gets a job working at the gallery, like a real paying job!"

"Don't you work at their diner, though?"

"Yeah, but anybody can do that job. If I left, they'd have it filled before the next day."

"Well, good for you! That'd be tremendous."

Aimee fishes a folded piece of paper from her back pocket. "Only thing is, I gotta have a school sponsor because of my age. So would it be okay if you sponsored me? It's just a form to fill out. You won't have to pay or anything."

"Of course, I'd be glad to." I smooth out the folds and grab a pen to write in my contact information and sign on the dotted line.

Refolding the form and shoving it back into her pocket, Aimee starts to say something and then stops herself. She does this several times and then looks down at the floor.

I sit back and fold my hands in my lap. "What's on your mind, kiddo?" I ask. "You know this is a safe place."

She takes a long breath. "So, remember when I was here the last time? I said that I was using Simon's legal aid rep to work on the emancipation process?"

"Yep, I do. So how's that going? Do you need anything from me?"

"No, not on that. The process is going good. But do you remember me saying that there might actually be a criminal case in the works that involved my last foster family?"

Kendra steps into the corner of the room, clipboard and pen ready to write.

A criminal case against Carl Blackwell! God in heaven, could that actually be true?

I clear my throat and nod. "Yes, I remember. Is that actually gonna move forward?"

Aimee fishes a business card from her other back pocket and slides it across the desk toward me. "So, I met last week with my legal aid rep for some more paperwork, and there was this lady there from the state prosecutor's office. She told me there was somebody inside child services who had come forward as a whistleblower against that family, and she wanted to know if I'd be willing to be interviewed and go on record for the criminal case they're planning to file."

My eyebrows shoot up. "And?"

Another deep breath. "So I said yes. She and I spent probably two hours together. I told her everything. Best part was that she believed me. She said if I wanted to, I might even have the chance to testify in court if it comes to that. But only if I feel like it. She said she could still use my interview as my testimony if I didn't want to appear in front of him in court. I haven't decided about that part yet."

Tiny Tot peeks around from behind Kendra. I motion him away with my hand.

Now is not the time to cry.

"Keep it together, man," warns the Bossman.

I sniff hard and sit up straight. "So was there a question you had for me about it?"

"Well, this lady said she's looking for someone who could act as a character witness for me, to back up my story and help show that I'm not a druggie or a nut job. She asked about school records, you know, absences and stuff that would line up with the same dates of some of the things that happened to me. So I was wanting to ask you if maybe you'd think about calling this lady and offering to be a witness?"

God, is this actually happening? All these years later, am I really going to see justice?

15

AGE FORTY-EIGHT

I sit on a poorly padded, orange and brown chevron cloth bench. It's probably been here since smoking was still legal indoors. Traipsing the stale halls, sharply dressed lawyers weave around plaintiffs and defendants—some frightened, some belligerent—all moving with equal parts determination. One for truth, the other for blood. It smells of despair and injustice in the dust.

I never knew jury selection proceedings were open to the public.

My offense and disdain for the judicial system has brought a semi-permanent snarl to my upper lip whenever I'm within a mile of a courthouse. Where were the champions of justice when I needed them? Bought and paid for with dirty money, every last one.

I wonder how many people who have found themselves in a pool of potential jurors have any clue how corrupt the system is? Do they have even the faintest idea of how many judges are either on the take, or are so deeply in cahoots with people on both sides that they can't even give directions to the bathroom honestly?

These incessant unanswerable questions swarm like bees in my brain as I sit in the hallway of the Commonwealth of Kentucky Court of Justice outside of Courtroom B.

As a witness for the prosecution, I'm not allowed to sit in on the jury selection proceedings. Just another arbitrary rule that limits fairness and truth. But, rules are rules, so here I sit. Reporters are permitted inside, though, and there's no law against live social media posts as long as jurors aren't identified. So I tolerate the dingy, stuffy hallway glued to several social media accounts, refreshing my feeds constantly.

Kendra stands in a corner across from me, counting ceiling tiles with her arms crossed.

The press has gone wild over this case. News anchors and beat reporters can't get enough of the bold teenage victim underdog, David-versus-Goliath story. From the moment Aimee's suit was filed under a collective of Jane Doe aliases, cameras and local television personalities from Cleveland to Nashville descended on the area like hyenas on a fresh kill. Every story is the same. Feigning sympathy, they report such shock and horror over the allegations. "How could an agency created to protect young children possibly have been involved in such atrocities?! Surely this hasn't ever happened before!"

News this interesting will make the jury selection much more difficult, so two hundred potential jurors have been summoned to appear in Courtroom B.

The law of the land guarantees a defendant the right to a trial by a jury of his peers. But the state of Kentucky is the defendant in this lawsuit, so I'm not sure it's technically possible to have a jury of peers. I cannot imagine that a true peer to the corrupt bureaucrats could ever side against their own.

Leaning back with my extra-large cold brew, my cell phone charger plugged in, I settle in for the play-by-play.

Aside from the desire to scope out the territory ahead of my potential testimony, I'm not exactly sure what compels me to be here. I'm just a minor witness in a major case. If I even take the stand, which is iffy at best, the attorneys have said my testimony is only to help establish more credibility for Aimee.

She is why I'm here. I have seen and heard so much of myself in her, and more than once my body has manifested its understanding of her pain and grief. Like war veterans with similar stories from different eras, we've shared a familiarity in the travesty of ongoing injustice.

As I was leaving the house this morning, Grace reached up to put both hands on my shoulders, "Are you trying to relive your own journey of betrayal through Aimee's?"

Perhaps so. I've admitted I envy this teenager's boldness and her courage to dig in, despite the powerful opposition against her.

At Aimee's age I was drinking and snorting myself into willful oblivion. She is much smarter than I was.

I glance at my mobile news feed. Twenty-five jurors have already been dismissed. The first social media post by one Jeffrey Moreland stationed inside the proceedings indicates that these twenty-five had been connected in some way to the state foster care system. A wave of cynicism washes over me.

The defense cannot possibly expect someone inside the system to have a single positive thing to say. Of course those people would be dismissed.

I smile at the next post by Jeffrey Moreland. "One of those

twenty-five was heard commenting as she exited, 'About time somebody held these people accountable.' Judge Jackson immediately warned the remaining pool to disregard the outburst, and that anyone making additional comments would be charged with contempt."

An almost imperceptible thought floats through my mind. "Have you thought about praying over this case?"

Looking around, I expect to find someone speaking. But there's only Kendra, and that was definitely not her voice.

Praying? About a court case? Ha! Yeah, right. As if that would do any good.

"What could it hurt?" the quiet voice challenges.

Ha! What could it hurt? False hopes, disappointment, more letdowns and a whole lot of nothing in response for starters.

The thought comes quickly. "But what if prayer actually did help?"

This has to be God speaking.

I scoff. "Ok, God, You want me to pray?" I say aloud under my breath. "Here's a prayer. Carl Blackwell deserves the death penalty. Could You make that happen? That's my prayer."

Not wanting to wait for an answer, I slurp down the last drops of my coffee just as I realize how uncomfortably full my bladder is. Tucking my phone and my keys in my pocket, I hustle toward the restrooms in the center courtroom atrium. A slight panic erupts as I come upon the massive trash can blocking the restroom and a sign that reads "Closed for Maintenance."

I start to do the cross-legged bathroom dance as I hurry

toward an armed guard near the elevator. Pain contorts my face.

"Sir, I hate to ask this," I say, breathless at my discomfort, "but I seriously need a restroom like ASAP. What's my fastest option?"

Checking his watch, the officer proceeds toward a small side door. "This way, sir, but make it quick. This hallway is usually reserved for people with security clearance." As he unlocks the door, I'm beyond grateful to see the clearly labeled men's room door halfway down the hall.

I make it to the urinal just in time. Relief floods me and the pain subsides as I let out a laughably long sigh.

Next time I don't need an extra-large!

After flushing the urinal and readjusting my pants, I move to the sink to wash my hands. Just as I start to lather up, three men walk through the door.

Carl Blackwell stands between two heavily armed police officers who proceed to unlock the wrist cuffs of their detainee. Carl and I lock eyes for a moment in the mirror, and it's clear he has no idea who I am. With his splotchy face, bloated waistline, and well-worn prison jumpsuit, Carl is a former shell of himself.

In an instant, an uncontrollable trembling overtakes my hands, and a dizzy, disorienting swirl of confusion and fear threatens to drop me to my knees. One part of me feels like a terrified five-year-old being threatened yet again by his tyrannical big brother. A much bigger part of me knows I'm a strong, healthy adult who would have no problem ending Carl's existence with my bare hands right now.

"Don't be a moron, Danny," warns the Bossman.

Brody catches my eye in the mirror as Carl, with his

ankles still shackled, shuffles over to a urinal. Taking a deep breath, I shake my head slightly at Brody to send him on his way. Drying my hands quickly with a few paper towels, I nod at the officers and head out the door.

I've had enough of this courtroom for today. I make my way out to my car, forcing myself to breathe in the spring air deeply so I can hold it together long enough to drive home.

Hey, God? My last prayer still stands.

16

AGE FORTY-EIGHT

How crazy can I possibly be?

Jenny Burkhardt, the lead prosecuting attorney in the class action case against the state of Kentucky, glares at me clench faced. "Do you actually expect me to believe you don't remember saying anything you just saw yourself say? How is that even possible, Mr. Pierce?"

Tears of shame threaten as I feel my face redden. "I wish I could answer that," I say. "I'm as confused as you are." The smallness of the conference room threatens to close in, and the musty smell of old courthouse carpet stings my nose.

Tiny Tot comes out from under the table and looks at me with a tear in his eye. But I don't want to be seen crying, so I shake my head at him and he goes back under the table.

"Do you realize I may have to start all over?" she asks, her volume rising. "You might even be charged with contempt!" Kendra stands over Jenny's shoulder, writing furiously.

The courtroom video replays over in my mind, but I have nowhere to put it.

God, I've called myself crazy for years, but am I going completely psycho?

This morning I had jumped out of bed early. I'd wanted to be clear headed and on time at the courthouse. It was my turn to take the stand as a witness in the class-action case that Aimee had joined against the state foster system.

I had hoped that perhaps for the first time in my life, I might get to see some kind of justice. I went out for a brisk, early walk, showered and shaved, and had a nice, quiet breakfast with Grace. She even prayed with me before I left for the courthouse.

After weaving through crowds and reporters anxious to get their scoop, Jenny and I met in a side conference room as planned. We had already rehearsed my testimony about Aimee several times over. Jenny had played the role of devil's advocate well as she practiced cross-examining me. So I felt confident and prepared for anything.

I was wrong.

As we walked into the courtroom, I was pleasantly surprised at how packed the place was. Then a tiny pang of nervousness hit me as I noticed Aimee sitting in the back row. Her thumbs-up gave me a boost, and by the time Jenny called me as a witness for the prosecution, I strode up to the podium and swore to tell the truth with ease. As I sat in the witness stand, the Bossman said, "You got this, Danny. Piece of cake."

My confidence was bolstered by the news that Carl Blackwell himself would not be present in the courtroom during this segment of the proceedings. Part of me was grateful. Part of me wanted to revel in the shackles around his hands and feet.

Jenny's questions went off exactly as we had rehearsed.

She took extra time to discuss my perceptions of Aimee's emotional and physical well-being as her school counselor, and we both knew that my responses would garner sympathy from the jury. Acutely aware of the need for as much jury sympathy as possible, Jenny milked the emotional questions and answers. She even included several well-timed, dramatic sighs and pained, grief-laden facial expressions.

Then it was the defense attorney's turn.

"Mr. Carlson," said Judge Jackson, the wiry, elderly fixture of county justice. "Your witness."

A cocky young man with Justin Bieber hair and an Armani suit took his time to saunter my direction, an open file folder in one hand.

"Mr. Pierce, is it?" he asked, eyes on his file.

"Yes," I answered, already disliking the man.

"Can you tell the court, please. How long have you been a school counselor?"

"So, I've been at Kingston High School for nine years," I said. "And before that I was at Fairhope Middle School in Choctaw County for two years. So, eleven years total."

Still looking at his folder, Carlson asked, "Can you explain to the court what it means to be a mandated reporter?"

I sat up, confident. "Sure. So if a child reveals something to a mandated reporter like myself, such as claims of abuse or violence, we're required under state law to report those statements to either child services or to Crimes Against Children, depending on the nature of the harm. So if the child reveals extreme neglect, or unsafe living conditions, or use of illicit drugs in the home, I would file a report to child services. If the child reported things related to themselves, like they're being sexually abused or suffering physical violence, I would report those to Crimes Against Children. If it's extreme then I would report to both."

Making a dramatic page turn, Carlson continued. "Mr. Pierce, do you know what the average number of child services referrals is for the average school counselor in the state of Kentucky?"

I glanced at Jenny. She stood immediately. "Objection, Your Honor. Relevance."

"I withdraw the question, Your Honor," Carlson replied. "The court would probably be interested to know that over the last twenty-five years, in the state of Kentucky, the average annual number of referrals to child services by school counselors across the state is twelve."

Garrison marched into the courtroom and came to stand at attention next to Jenny.

"So, Mr. Pierce," Carlson continued. "Can you tell the court what your average number of child services referrals has been in the eleven years since you became a school counselor?"

Carlson finally looked at me, smirking. Kendra scribbled on her clipboard behind him, as usual. The dusty, stale air made me sweaty, and I was thankful when an air conditioner kicked on somewhere to start blowing coolness around the room.

I took a moment to respond. "I, uh, I haven't counted them up, so I–…"

"Let me help your memory, Mr. Pierce. Over the last eleven years, you have managed to average fifty referrals to Child Protective Services every year. In the last twelve months alone, you made over sixty referrals."

Jenny stood again. "Objection."

Judge Jackson looked small in his big black robe, but his voice carried authority. "Mr. Carlson, if you don't establish relevance to this case, I'll be forced to sustain Ms. Burkhardt's objection."

"Indeed, Your Honor," said Carlson with a slight bow. "My purpose here is to establish that this witness has his own personal vendetta against the defendants in this case, and I intend to clearly show how his documented actions provide evidence of bias."

Glancing at the exit doors as I gripped the wooden edge of the witness box, I resisted the urge to bolt.

More smirking from Carlson. He traipsed slowly before the jury as his questions continued, never looking at me. "Isn't it true, Mr. Pierce, that you yourself were a child served by this very same foster care system? And isn't it true that as an adult, your plan to punish the system you didn't like now includes referring case after baseless case for investigation? And isn't it true, Mr. Pierce, that close to seventy percent of the cases you have referred to child services over the years have all been dismissed as baseless and unverifiable? Do you expect the jury to believe that you're the only school counselor in the entire state of Kentucky with some kind of superhuman gift of discernment to correctly identify when a child is at risk? Or is every child alive today actually being abused, Mr. Pierce?!"

Instantly suffocated, I looked at Jenny again.

"Objection, Your Honor! Badgering the witness!"

The room began to grow misty, and I felt a hot uprising from my gut as I looked at Carlson. As he smirked at me, his face contorted ever so slightly. I found myself looking at what my mind believed was a sneering teenage Carl Blackwell, the sociopathic redheaded son of Butch and Gina.

I know I blacked out at that point, because I had to watch everything that followed on video later. I could not believe what I saw myself say and do.

"You like little boys, don't you Carl?" I asked, leaning forward with an unfriendly smile. The voice wasn't my normal, late-forties aged voice. I sounded much younger, and much angrier.

My eyes narrowed, and my lips contorted into a menacing snarl. "You know what you like to do, you little pervert. You like to hurt little kids and make videos, that's what you like to do."

Carlson's shocked expression didn't register as I continued.

"You like to lock little boys in the basement and make them scream in the dark." I patted my chest. "How about me, Carl? Wanna try and hurt me now? C'mon." I rose up from the witness stand chair. "Hurt me now, big man!" I screamed from the top of my lungs. "Come and get a piece of Brody!"

The judge banged his gavel emphatically several times. "Counsel, control your witness!" he boomed.

Carlson raised his hands and laughed. "Your Honor, I move to strike the entire testimony of this witness on the grounds of mental illness and clear confusion. This must also be considered as we negotiate bail for my client." He laughed again and took his seat. "This guy's nuts."

I continued to challenge and threaten who my mind believed was Carl Blackwell under my breath as a huge bailiff grabbed my elbow and escorted me out a side door.

I came back to my senses in the conference room again, to a very angry Jenny.

"What's... what's going on?" I asked her as awareness returned. "Why are we in here?" A sick, sinking feeling hit my stomach.

"You tell me!" she retorted. "What was all that back there, calling Mr. Carlson 'Carl?' And telling him he likes little boys! What in God's name was that? And who is Brody?!"

I slumped backward and let out a deep sigh.

Brody is my fighter. But I can't tell her that.

I raised my hands. "I'm sorry. I have no idea what just happened. I feel like I blacked out."

"Oh yeah?" She ripped open her laptop and scrolled through a few screens. "Well, here is exactly what you just missed."

Now fully present again, I watch the grainy CCTV video in horror as I see myself become someone else entirely.

How crazy can I possibly be?

Kendra is busy writing in the corner.

Jenny slams her laptop shut and stands to leave. "I don't know what's going on with you, Mr. Pierce, but obviously I have to release you as a witness. For Aimee's sake, I need to advise you to stay away from her. Send her to another counselor if you have to. But you're not to discuss this case with her, or with anyone else who might be connected. You'll be lucky if you don't lose your job. Do I make myself clear?"

She puts one hand on the doorknob and pauses. "From what I saw in there, Mr. Pierce, I highly suggest you get some serious help."

I don't even know where to begin.

17

AGE FORTY-EIGHT

The vibration of the cell phone in my pocket creates a welcome distraction from the crippling boredom of this annual school planning meeting. I've bitten my lip multiple times for the past two hours to stop myself from groaning out loud while everyone argues about relay races, colored pencils, and whether hiring a hypnotist for the fall carnival is crossing some line.

I slide the phone from my pocket to peek at the screen. "Sunset Ridge Franklin" appears on the caller ID.

Gypsy.

Slipping out a side door, I tiptoe into the quiet hallway. "Y-y-yes? This is Danny Pierce," I answer. My throat is instantly dry and my heart pounds. Garrison, Kendra, and Tiny Tot appear in front of me.

The gentle voice on the line answers.

"Are you Daniel James Pierce, the son of Elizabeth Belle Nicholson who was born on October 6, 1944, in Cincinnati, Ohio?"

"That's correct."

"Hello, Mr. Pierce. My name is Nina Marlowe. Are you in a place where we can speak for a moment?"

"Yes, ma'am, can I help you?"

"Mr. Pierce, I'm the assistant director at Sunset Ridge senior care village down here in Franklin. You probably know that we've been taking care of your mother—she has us call her Gypsy—for the last twelve years."

I try to answer, but only dry air comes out. I clear my throat. "Yes, ma'am."

She takes a long breath. "Mr. Pierce, these calls are never easy, and I'm sorry to be the one to deliver this kind of news. But I wanted to let you know that Miss Gypsy passed away in her sleep last night."

Thankful that I'm leaning against the wall, my legs buckle. Bending my knees, I slide down the wall to sit on the floor. Tiny Tot comes to sit beside me.

What am I supposed to feel right now?

"Okay," I say. "Umm…" No other words will come.

"Mr. Pierce, all of your mother's paperwork is in order. She had everything taken care of, and everything is already paid for. In her final directive, she gave us all of the instructions we needed to handle her arrangements and cremation. So there's really nothing that we need from you. We'll be mailing you a copy of the arrangement details."

"Mm-hmm," I mumble in response, brushing away an unexpected tear rolling down my cheek. Tiny Tot sniffs and wipes his face with his sleeve.

"Mr. Pierce, Miss Gypsy did leave a letter for you, but I need to confirm the mailing address that we have on file for you."

I'm assaulted by disturbing mental images of Gypsy's long, wavy black hair burning in a fiery coffin. I pound my forehead with the palm of my hand to turn off the horror movie. Shaking my head, I blink hard and push myself back up onto my feet. "Yes, of course," I say. "The address is 312 Baxter Court, Georgetown, Kentucky 40320."

Nina Marlowe reads the address back to me and then clears her throat. "Mr. Pierce, I'm not sure if you're a man of faith, but sometimes we can find comfort by turning to a greater power than ourselves in times like these."

I mumble something similar to a thanks.

A lot of comfort He's been for me lately. And now He takes my mom? Some comfort He is!

The jarring school bell and the chatter of students pouring out of classroom doors barely register as I shuffle back to my office with the phone to my ear. Tiny Tot, Garrison, and Kendra follow close behind. Nina promises to place the letter in the mail today and thanks me for my time.

"Mr. Pierce," she says. "I'm so very sorry for the loss of your mother. We've all become quite fond of Miss Gypsy over the years. We're truly gonna miss her around here. Please do call me at this number if you need anything at all."

Tapping the screen to end the call and falling into my chair, I drop the phone and bury my head into my hands.

How can I possibly be grieving this mother I barely knew, the woman who abandoned me?

"Mama is dead?" Tiny Tot's voice breaks as his childlike question sends new pain through my heart. Meeting his gaze, I nod my head and open up my arms. We both start to weep as he climbs up into my lap and I sink into blissful darkness.

18

AGE FIFTEEN

I am fifteen years old, and my real mother sees invisible people.

She's crazier than I am.

After three city bus changes and a half-mile walk across four blocks and a bridge, I sit across from Gypsy in her room at Havencrest State Psychiatric Hospital.

"Do you know where they took my baby boy?" she slurs. "Some people came and took him away and I can't find him. He can't sleep without his green lovey blanket." Her black hair wild and matted, Gypsy tries to get up off of the hospital bed, but her arms and legs are restrained with heavy leather straps buckled to the railing. A sickening aroma of bleach mixed with urine fills the room, and the stained, tattered window blinds cast a dingy yellow tone over everything. It's unlikely she would have alcohol in here, but I wonder if she's drunk just the same.

My response is cut off as she jerks her head to glare over

her shoulder at the wall. "Hush! I'm talking right now! You can talk when I'm finished!"

There's no one there.

"Who are you talking to?" I ask. Kendra stands in the corner ready to write.

Gypsy flops her head back down onto the pillow and huffs. "That's Billy," she says. "He never shuts up. Sometimes I like it, but sometimes he makes up stories. Like right now he's trying to tell me that you're my baby boy who loves his blanket."

Cocking her head to one side, she stares through me for several quiet moments. Giving a slight laugh, she shakes her head. "But that couldn't possibly be right. You're almost a grown man." Eyes closed and chin tilted upward, she breathes so deeply I wonder if she's fallen asleep.

She turns her head slowly to stare out the cloudy window. "Those green tractors get me every time, you know?" The pitch of her voice has changed, the drunk-sounding drawl replaced with mature clarity and wisdom.

My brows furrow.

She continues, but in the high-pitched voice of a young girl. "Why is this old tractor even in here, Uncle Charlie? You don't have a big field to plow."

Gypsy mimics the sound of an older man speaking to a child. "'Oh, that belongs to your grandpaw. It was his daddy's before the war. It might be worth something someday.'" The little girl's voice speaks again. "There's Grandpaw now. Hey, come play with me and Uncle Charlie in the barn!"

She shrinks into herself as fear twists her face. "No, Grandpaw, I don't want to hide under the sheet, it's yucky and dark in here. Uncle Charlie, what are you doing? Please can I go back home? That hurts, please let me go home, I promise I won't tell…"

I force myself to swallow the vomit rising in my throat.

Squeezing her eyes shut and taking several deep breaths, Gypsy straightens her shoulders. She gazes out the window again. The clear-headed adult voice returns. "That green tractor with the yellow trim was burned into my mind every time they took me in that barn. Been almost forty years now, but whenever I see that little green and yellow tractor picture on somebody's baseball hat, or on a T-shirt, or even on television, everything shuts down and I fall into a black hole I can't explain."

Goose bumps cover my skin.

I've also known my own black hole I can't explain.

She turns to face me, her eyes clear and focused. "You got any idea what that's like?"

I lean forward, elbows on my knees. "Well, you might not believe this, but I actually do have an idea of what that's like."

"It's frustrating, not knowing how long I'll be gone before I come back into my head again. Sometimes it's just a couple hours. Once it was almost a whole year. When I finally made it back to my place, somebody else was living there and all my stuff was gone."

Sadness had crept into her tone, but her eye contact told me she was still present.

"Wow, that's a long time," I say. "It's usually just an hour or two when that happens to me."

A quizzical look crosses her face. "What did you say your name was again?"

I take a deep breath. "My name is Danny. I'm your son. I'm Danielle's little brother."

She inhales sharply and tears begin to pool as her eyebrows shoot up. Her voice cracks as she whispers, "D..D...Danny?"

My heart pounds as I stand up and move to sit beside her on the bed and take hold of the one hand I can reach.

I'm not gonna cry. I'm NOT gonna cry.

Weeping freely, eyes still locked to mine, Gypsy giggles. "You're so big! How old are you?"

I grin. "Just turned fifteen."

At my answer, a wave of pain crosses her face, but she shakes it off. "Wow, that went by real fast. How were you able to find me here?"

"Well, I was helping my mom, sorry, I mean the mom who adopted me, I was helping her clean out some old boxes and we found my birth certificate. She said she didn't care if I tried to find you. We don't have the greatest relationship."

"That stinks, sorry."

"Yeah, so I just went to the phone book. Not a lot of other people with your same name, so I just started calling around. One lady who answered said that she was your cousin, and that you used to live there. Then she told me you were here. I took the bus."

My heart swells at the light and love pouring from her face as she looks at me. "So, you got anything you wanna know?" she asks gently.

I shrug. "I don't know. Everything, I guess."

We talk for over an hour. I learn that she had lived and worked in the busiest brothel in Lexington, and it was there she became known as Gypsy Belle. Big Nana, a rough and powerful woman, ran the place like a Marine sergeant. She had discovered sixteen-year-old Gypsy half-dead behind a dumpster and nursed her back to health in exchange for her service of the never-ending brothel clients. But Big Nana had never seen such bad mental illness. When Gypsy would slip into the void, Big Nana would have to let her ride out the storm here at Havencrest. She was here so often that Gypsy had a special fast check-in pass.

Eventually Big Nana discovered which drugs would help Gypsy keep working without going crazy. It worked most of the time, and clients mattered more than addiction.

According to Gypsy, abortion was the norm for Big Nana's girls. The second anyone suspected a pregnancy, Big Nana called her cousin, a hawk-nosed doctor whose license had been revoked, to pay a late-night visit to take care of the problem.

But at least twice, Gypsy's pregnancies went undetected until she had progressed too far along. She knew Big Nana would force her to scrub pots at her brother's diner if she couldn't work at the brothel. So she stayed at Havencrest through her entire pregnancy with me.

This is how I learn that I began my life in an insane asylum, born to an addicted, mentally ill prostitute.

I sit in stunned silence. Kendra writes furiously over in the corner.

Tilting her chin and raising her brows, she asks with pink cheeks, "Too much all at once?"

"Nah, it's not that. I mean, it's pretty heavy stuff. But..."

"But what?"

"The thing about falling into a black hole you can't explain. I do know what that's like."

Her pained expression hurts my heart. She squeezes my hand. "Oh, I'm so sorry. Are you seeing doctors or anything?"

I snort. "Nah. I'll be alright."

Poor people like me don't go to a doctor.

Soft tears continue to slide down her cheeks. "Danny, will you look at me?"

The love from her crystal blue eyes disarms me. I want to look away but I don't.

"Sweetie, I am real sorry that I couldn't be there for you."

No one has ever called me sweetie.

A deep pain begins to swell up from my belly. I can only nod and bite the inside of my cheek.

"When you lived with me at Big Nana's, I was making plans for us. She was letting me save up some money so we could get a little place of our own. She was even gonna let me get my G.E.D. so we could start over."

She pauses to look out the window again and takes a deep breath. "One day when you was almost four, I had a john I never seen before. What a jerk he was, swaggering and boasting about some job he had with the county. So I take care of business for him, and he's getting dressed and you woke up scared and came in my room. Soon as he saw you, it's like he flipped a switch. Started going on about how I'm an unfit mother, and how could I have a kid and be a whore. I wasn't gonna let any john talk to me like that, especially in front of you, so I yelled at him. Biggest mistake of my life. That man beat me so bad I was knocked out the whole night. When I woke up, you and Danielle was gone. Turns out he worked for child services. The next day I got served with papers that said my parental rights had been cut off. I never saw either one of you again."

I have no idea what to do with the pain surging through my chest. I wonder if my heart may actually explode.

Movement in the corner catches my eye. Kendra is still writing, but there's a little boy standing in front of her. He looks like a four-year-old version of me, and he's crying.

Gypsy turns her head in the direction of the little boy and her brows furrow for a quick moment.

Did she just see him, too? That's not possible.

She closes her eyes with a pained wince and turns back toward me.

"This is Tiny Tot," Kendra barks at me. "He's the only one who is allowed to cry now."

Gypsy reaches up to cup my cheek in her hand. "Is there any way that you can forgive me, Danny?"

I start to answer as a nurse barges in. "Time for your medication, Miss Nicholson," the lady calls in a sing-song lilt.

At the mention of the promised drug, the bright-eyed connection with my mom vanishes, replaced by the slurring, detached persona of a broken mental patient.

Gypsy giggles at the nurse like a toddler in a candy store as I slip back into the chair. Downing the pills with a small cup of water, she rests back on the pillow with closed eyes. The pills work fast. A goofy grin forms on her face, and she looks in my direction.

"Do you know where they took my baby boy?" she slurs again. "Some people came and took him away and I can't find him."

Before I can answer, Tiny Tot climbs up onto Gypsy's bed and curls up in a ball, his head tucked into her hair, nuzzled into the crook of her neck. He starts to calm down.

She laughs with delight. "Well there you are, sweet boy!" she says, grinning with a strange sparkle in her eyes. "Oh, I've missed you so much, my baby!"

The restraint straps prevent her from wrapping her arms all the way around him. One hand strokes the back of his little head, and the other hand wraps gently around his foot. "Mommy's here," she coos. "Mommy has you."

Agony erupts from my belly as I vaguely remember snuggling into that hair. Peeking out from under Gypsy's chin, Tiny Tot locks eyes with me as I slump back in my chair and give in to the black.

19

AGE FORTY-EIGHT

My wife is gonna kill me.

If I don't kill myself first.

I think seriously about several viable options to end my life as quickly as possible with the least amount of mess to clean up. But as I envision my family grieving at my funeral, I smack myself in the face.

You can't do that to them. Don't be an idiot.

"You're fine, Danny," adds the Bossman. "It happens. It's just a suspension. If they end up firing you, you'll find another job. They're a bunch of clueless losers anyway. Stop overreacting."

His reminder of the fact that I have just been suspended with partial pay just before the new year punches me in the gut again.

Superintendent Ragsdale had heard about my meltdown in court. But he had also heard about the case referral numbers comparison that the defense attorney had thrown in my face.

Before I could finish my first cup of coffee earlier this

morning, he and Principal Miller had knocked on my door and walked right into my office. Tanner Pike, the ambitious hotshot human resources coordinator, walked in with them, massive policies and procedures handbook tucked under his arm.

"Danny, we need to have a serious discussion," said Ragsdale. His cheeks were red and his eyes flashed with anger. He reminded me of a salty Santa Claus. Principal Miller seemed to cower behind Ragsdale.

My heart sank. The presence of Tanner Pike could only mean one thing. Kendra stood behind them in the corner, recording every word.

"Am I being fired?" I asked, almost too quiet to be heard.

Ragsdale ignored my question. "Danny, it's been brought to my attention that you agreed to help a student by becoming involved in a criminal case where the student is working with the DA's office for prosecution of a crime. I assume that's true?"

For a split second, I was back on that witness stand being cross-examined by a jerk.

I cleared my throat. "Yes, sir, that's correct. Aimee Dixon. She was approached directly by an attorney handling the case, and she asked me to serve as a character witness to help corroborate her story. It made sense, given that I've been counseling her for several months. I'm probably one of the few adults in the world who actually knows her entire story and the impact it's had on her life."

Tanner Pike spoke up, his nasally voice grating and loud. "Mr. Pierce, are you aware that you have violated school system policy by doing that?"

Slapping open his massive three-ring binder onto the desk in front of me, he crossed his arms and huffed.

A lump rose in my throat as I read the section of the handbook marked by a yellow sticky note with a huge black arrow pointing to my crime. "School system staff must receive advanced written clearance from the district superintendent prior to discussing student matters outside of the school system. This requirement includes, but is not limited to: civil or criminal court agents; attorneys or other legal representatives; members of the medical community; or members of the press."

I sat back, pinching the bridge of my nose. "Oh, wow, I had absolutely no idea that was in there. I really thought I was helping and doing the right thing. She didn't have anyone else to help."

Tanner Pike slapped another piece of paper down in front of me. "Is this your signature?" he asked. The document labeled "School System Staff Policies Handbook Acknowledgement" was clearly signed by me.

I held the page in my hands and noticed the fine print. "By my signature below, I acknowledge it is my responsibility to read and understand this handbook. I further understand that violations of the policies within this handbook will result in my being subject to disciplinary action, including suspension, demotion, reassignment, or termination of my employment."

Sliding the page back toward Tanner, I answered, "Yes, it appears so."

Satisfied with his conviction, Tanner retrieved the handbook and the acknowledgment form and sat in one of the chairs across from me. Ragsdale remained standing.

"If that weren't enough, Mr. Pierce," Ragsdale continued,

"what is this I hear about the excessive number of child services referrals coming out of this office?"

Defeated and empty, I held my palms out. "I'm trying to help the kids that no one else will help, sir. I know what it's like to be them. Principal Miller, you've seen some of those file notes. Can you help me out here?"

Miller shrank even more behind Ragsdale, her eyes fixed to the ground without an answer.

Ragsdale held up a file folder. "According to our counts, you're still spending way too much time in your one-on-ones. We've talked about this. In order to meet the state standards, you're supposed to have a daily average of eight open student time slots. Do you know what your average is, Mr. Pierce?"

I started to answer, but Ragsdale answered for me. "I'll tell you how many. Three point five sessions. Less than half!"

Standing, I meet his angry gaze. "Maybe if the county hired another counselor, we could actually have meaningful time with these kids instead of shuffling them through like burgers at a fast-food counter. And adding your data reporting project onto my plate certainly didn't help with my schedule. With all due respect, *sir*." My emphasis on "sir" was most definitely not respectful.

Ragsdale inched forward, his chest puffed. "But despite your low productivity as a counselor, you manage to refer fifty-some cases to child services a year, when the state average is a dozen? Mr. Pierce, you have seriously damaged the reputation of this school and this county. Some of these kids don't need child services or a counselor. What some of them need is to be spanked and grounded until they learn to behave themselves."

I crossed my arms. "I could not disagree more, sir. Apparently you didn't have to fight for your life as a kid like a lot of these kids have to do. I know what it's like. They deserve to be heard and believed, not smacked around. In fact, sir, it offends me to hear you say that."

"I have zero interest in your offense, Mr. Pierce. You have clearly violated written policy. You have embarrassed my office, and you have been in opposition to the goals and standards of this department for years. We have no choice but to place you on an indefinite suspension effective immediately. We will conduct our own internal investigation as soon as the January classes resume, and the school board will make a decision about your employment whenever that investigation is complete. Tanner will accompany you as you remove your personal belongings. And under no circumstances are you to have any contact with any student in this district, especially Aimee Dixon. I trust I make myself explicitly clear!"

Turning on his heel, Ragsdale strode from my office with Principal Miller close behind. Brody came into the room, but I shook my head at him.

The last thing I need in here is a fight.

Standing with a flourish, Tanner Pike nodded at my desk with a satisfied smirk.

It took less than four minutes to collect my sad handful of picture frames, loose change, and other personal effects.

Now I drive mindlessly for several hours, afraid to go home and face Grace with what I've done. I decide to tell her the bad news over the dinner we've planned at Luigi's. At least I'll have the safety of a crowd around me to minimize the chances of a big scene. Over and over I mull the verbiage I plan to use as I break the news to Grace until something inside me pops.

"God, why are You doing this to me?!" I scream at the top of my lungs while waiting for a red light to change.

A soft and gentle thought reaches me. "Danny, this isn't My doing."

"Oh yeah?! Well whose doing is it then, huh?"

"There's an enemy of your soul, Danny, who came to steal, kill, and destroy."

I scoff. "Yeah, but apparently You're supposed to be more powerful and omnipotent and sovereign and all of that. I know You saved me from hell, and I am grateful for that. But is that all there is? I get my fire insurance and then You ditch and watch me suffer from a distance? Whole lotta good it's doing for me now. I'm trying to help kids like I was never helped, and this is the thanks I get?! So thanks for a whole lot of nothing!"

Rolling down my window to let the frigid December air blow, I ignore Kendra writing furiously in the back seat as I tune my radio to a classic rock station. Cranking up the volume, I sing overly loud with The Rolling Stones to distract myself.

It will be a miracle if my wife doesn't leave me.

20

AGE FORTY-EIGHT

S harp pain blazes through my jaw as I wake, my mouth half-open and full of cold sand. Nothing looks or smells familiar as I breathe deeply and spit. The grit that rubs against my teeth makes me wonder if I've swallowed a brick. I wipe my bottom lip and wince at the oozing gash on my chin. The sound of flowing water presses into my consciousness. A seeping dread comes over me as my faculties start to return.

I've checked out again.

"My name is Daniel James Pierce," I begin to recite aloud, grasping for the few brain cells that seem to be working. "I live at 312 Baxter Court. I'm married to my wife Grace, and..." *Grace!*

The sudden pounding in my chest shoots up painfully through my chin as I scramble to my feet and look around frantically for my wife. I recognize that I'm under an overpass along the North Elkhorn River, but I have no idea how I got here.

Think! THINK!! When did I see her last? Early dinner.

Pasta. Luigi's. We drove separately. Why can't I remember the end of dinner?

I look for the late afternoon sun to be to my right in the western sky. It's not visible on the horizon.

Why is that side of the sky so dark?

It looks like it's... Trembling, I glance at my watch. *This can't be right. It's seven-thirty... in the morning?!*

Stop. Breathe. Ground. Looking around, a stone bench comes into view. I stumble toward it as an icy gust of wind swirls the dead leaves around me. Recognizing my surroundings, I fight to understand how I'm at the edge of the River-walk Park.

Starting to hyperventilate, I collapse on the bench. *Tap the vagus nerve.* My hands cupped over my face, I inhale slowly through my nose. *Count backward. Tap eyebrows. Breathe. Tap temples. Breathe. Tap chin.* My panic begins to dissipate with the ritual performance of the steps I've learned from self-help gurus on social media. It eases the trembling somewhat, but it doesn't help the fear.

I hold a long breath, then release it slowly. *I need to get home.* Patting all of my pockets, my frustration mounts as I realize my cell phone is missing. I limp around in a widening circle, hunting for my cell phone with no luck. As I walk, the dirt on my clothes becomes more evident, and I wipe in disgust at the leaves and mud. *Is that a cigarette burn on my pants?* Shame washes over me at how awful I must look.

Glancing around, I see a crumpled beer can and several cigarette butts on the ground near where I woke up, but no phone. I start scrambling up the overpass embankment as the sun starts to crest over the trees across the river behind me. Still unsure how I ended up here, the sound of increasing rush-hour traffic greets my ears from the roadway above. Every step hurts, the chilly winter wind adding to the pain. My head is pounding, and nausea tries to creep up from my gut.

A slight sense of relief welcomes me as the outline of my car comes into view. It's parked in the gravel turnaround just before the overpass. I cannot help but wonder what the passing drivers must be thinking as they see me on all fours in the grass by the road.

I reach the back bumper of the car. A small punch hits my stomach as I realize that the front end of the car is resting against a guardrail post. I have clearly hit the railing. Checking the damage to the front end, I shake my head. *Great.* One headlight is smashed, and there's a small dent in the front quarter panel. Still, it should be drivable.

My front door is slightly ajar, but there doesn't appear to be anyone inside. Taking a long, steadying breath, I open the door fully and slide in. The keys are still in the ignition. "Thank You, God," I whisper out of habit.

The air inside reeks of stale beer and cigarette smoke. *Who has been in my car smoking and drinking?!* A sudden need to puke surges from my stomach, but I swallow hard and will it away. A glint catches my eye. I lean over to the passenger floorboard and grab my phone. The low battery light flashes red as I tap the screen. There are seventeen missed calls from Grace. Just as my finger taps the phone icon to call her back, the display goes black as the phone dies completely.

The rising sun blinds me, so I reach into my shirt pocket expecting my sunglasses. My fingers find a crumpled piece of paper instead. Opening it up, I cock my head to one side, my brow furrowed. It's a receipt for a twelve-pack of beer and a pack of cigarettes.

A sweaty chill creeps over my body as I look around inside my car. Crumpled beer cans litter the back seat and floorboard, and I see cigarette butts protruding from several of the cans. There's one beer can in the front cupholder. Picking it up and giving it a shake, I peer down into the open, mostly empty can. The stale smell of ash and beer violently assaults my senses, and I barely manage to turn back toward my open door before my stomach erupts onto the gravel.

My body spent from heaving, my temples pounding, I have trouble accepting the obvious conclusion of what has happened. I, Danny Pierce, the caring school counselor and good Christian father who never, ever touches alcoholic beverages, am embarrassingly hung over.

Tiny Tot climbs from the back seat to sit up front beside me. A painful, wailing scream surges out of my lungs, and tears begin to blur my vision. *How did I?! How could I?! THIS ISN'T WHO I AM!!!*

My thoughts are so scrambled, I don't notice the flashing blue lights atop the police car that pulls up behind me. Tiny Tot scrambles into the back seat as a stern voice interrupts my confused wailing.

"Sir, I'm gonna need for you to step out of the vehicle for me, please."

"Y..y..yes, sir," I stammer like a ten-year-old caught with stolen candy. Stepping around the mess on the ground, I lean against the side of the car.

I AM A GROWN CHRISTIAN MAN WITH A JOB AND CHILDREN! How is this my life right now?

The officer's words are muffled in my ears as I realize the

scene in front of him—a car full of empty beer cans wrecked into a guardrail, and a mud-covered wacko screaming like a little girl with the keys still in the ignition.

His voice cuts through my despair. "Sir? Sir, can you hear me?"

My eyes are fixed on the dirt. "Yes, sir."

"Sir, can you tell me what happened here?"

Looking around and into the car, I can taste the shame as I answer meekly. "I really don't know, officer."

He points to my car. "Is this your vehicle?"

"Yes, sir," I mumble.

"Were you driving this vehicle when it hit the guardrail?"

"I honestly don't remember, sir. I woke up on the ground down the embankment near the water, and I just climbed back up here."

He straightens. "Do you have any sort of identification, sir?"

I feel my back pocket where my wallet should be. Nothing. "I'm not sure, officer. It may be in the car somewhere. Is it okay if I look around for it?" My gaze is still fixed on the ground.

"What's your name, sir?"

"My name is Daniel James Pierce. I live at 312 Baxter Court. I'm married to my wife Grace, and..." Shifting my weight, a sharp, stabbing pain shoots down from my knee. I stifle a yelp.

"Sir, are you injured? Do you need medical attention?"

My cheeks flush. "I think I'm okay. I guess I'm just banged up a little."

The officer flips open a notepad. "Sir, can you tell me when this happened?"

Tears of helplessness threaten to erupt.

Why am I being such a baby?

"I don't know, officer. Last thing I can remember, I was having an early dinner with my wife. We met at Luigi's after work, but I'm drawing a blank after that."

Wait... Luigi's, Grace... oh yeah, I was suspended from work with only partial pay.

"How much alcohol did you have at dinner, sir?"

I look him in the face. "None!" I sound more defensive than I mean to. "I actually don't drink at all. I had sweet tea and she had a diet soda."

The officer's gaze goes from my face to the mess in my car and back again.

My heart races. "I know what it looks like, sir. But as God is my witness, I have no idea how all of that got into my car."

"Sir, do I have your consent to conduct a breathalyzer test?" He doesn't sound like he's giving me a choice.

Helplessness threatens to push tears from my eyes as I slump down into a squat. "Sure," I mumble. With my eyes closed to quell the sharp pain in my head, the next moments rush past in a blur. The officer's hand lifting me by my triceps shakes me back to reality.

"Mr. Pierce, you are under arrest for driving under the influence, for public intoxication, for having open alcoholic containers in your vehicle, and for leaving the scene of an accident." Cold steel closes around my wrist. *How is this really happening?!*

My shame will not be contained any longer, and I erupt into tears.

God? Are You there?! Oh God, what have I done? I can't handle this without You!

As the officer guides me into the back seat of his police cruiser, while completing his required speech about my Miranda rights, Garrison is already inside waiting for me. His arms crossed, his jaw set, he stares ahead with Tiny Tot sitting in his lap. Kendra is in the front seat. She's turned around facing me with a judgmental smirk, clipboard in hand.

I slump forward against the plexiglass partition in front of me, sobbing. "My life is over," I mumble.

Kendra badgers me. "What will the teachers at work think, Daniel? What about the people at church? At Grace's Bible study? What will Josiah and Abigail think about their sorry excuse of a father? What are the dads at the soccer field going to say about you?"

Her accusations bring a temporary halt to my blubbering. *What will people think?! GOD, I NEED YOU!!*

The officer slides into the front seat, buckles up, starts the car, and pulls into traffic. Garrison speaks, still staring straight ahead. "I won't let anything happen to you."

The world fades from gray to black as I check out into the void.

21

AGE FORTY-NINE

I chew my thumbnail as my eyes dart from the exit door to the restroom door to the large window. The waiting room chair is hard and the metal armrests poke my wrists and hips at the same time.

Every fiber of my being wants to run.

I wonder if there's a window in the bathroom that opens?

The Bossman chastises me. "You've been to this shrink three times, Danny. You're fine. Calm down, man. There's no need to make a scene. The guy didn't bite you before and he won't bite now. Don't be such a baby."

The Bossman's words divert my attention as my cheeks flush.

"I told you not to call me that," I growl in a whisper through gritted teeth. I glance around the room to ensure no one is watching. "I'm not a baby. Don't call me a baby."

His tone softens slightly. "Okay, okay. But don't act like you weren't just sitting here deciding which way out would be easier."

Busted.

I flop backward in my chair and cross my legs as my knee starts bouncing. Grace settles into the chair next to me and places a hand on my knee.

"You good?" she asks. "You seem a little jumpy."

I know she doesn't mean to accuse, but I'm already defensive.

"Nope. It's all fine," I mock. "Everything's fine and dandy. I just love being flayed open by a shrink."

Grace stares at me for a few seconds before turning to the year-old home décor magazine on the table in front of us. I'm thankful she doesn't respond.

Knowing that I need to be here doesn't make it any easier. In my mind's eye, a giant neon sign flashes "LOSER" over my head for the world to see.

I suppose "loser" is better than "drunk," which is the whole reason I'm here in the first place. I can still taste the mouthful of shame.

"Daniel Pierce?" A bubbly, rosy-cheeked receptionist pokes her head out from an interior door.

Great. My turn.

Immediately the Bossman speaks up. "You got this, Danny-boy. Easy peasy. Humor the guy, you know what he wants to hear. In and out. Piece of cake."

As Grace takes my hand, I find the Bossman hard to believe today.

We step into the same therapist's office we have visited for the last three weeks. As before, it reeks of brokenness. The sofa Grace and I share promises way more comfort than it delivers, and the dingy window shades evoke the same sadness and despair I sense oozing from every corner of the poorly-lit room.

Kendra is waiting for us already, clipboard and pen in hand.

Neil Schultz, our designated family therapist, slides his protruding belly behind his desk and eases carefully into his seat, fresh cup of coffee in hand. He takes a noisy slurp.

"Danny! Grace! Good to see you both again." He's almost too sincere. "How's it been going?"

I raise my hands in praise. "Well, the biggest news is that I've been granted first offender leniency in my DUI case, which is a miracle in itself. So instead of months in jail and thousands of dollars in fines, it's just probation and community service."

His eyes light up. "Really? That's fantastic news. I didn't think they did that anymore."

"Yeah, we didn't either," Grace answers. "We've been on our knees for weeks asking God for favor, and He heard us."

"Amen to that!" Neil pauses to look directly into my eyes for an uncomfortable moment. "So, tell me. How are things with you at home?"

Neil already had my file open on his desk, and he adds notes as Grace responds for us both.

I'm happy to have her answer about my apparent mood swings, although sometimes I have trouble seeing those. Then there's my meltdown three days ago after I started a fight with Grace about the six new pairs of men's shoes I found in the closet. I was absolutely certain there was no way I bought them. I'm not a spender like that. But apparently I can't remember anything from lunchtime onward Monday after getting an oil change for the car. And it turns out that my signature is right there on the shoe store receipt.

I am definitely going crazy. Who spends five hundred dollars on shoes and doesn't remember it? Me, apparently.

Steepling his fingers together and leaning back, Neil stares off into space to ponder Grace's update. His silence is threatening, but I'm unsure why.

Eventually he looks through several pages in my file. Then he leans forward with his elbows on the desk.

"Okay, Danny. Based on everything Grace is sharing, it sounds like you're dissociating. Do you know what that word means?"

I'm not an idiot.

Garrison walks in to stand beside Kendra.

"Yes," I answer. "It means to check out psychologically from a traumatic situation. But I didn't have what you'd call trauma at work Monday. Just a quarterly staff planning meeting that they demanded I attend even though I'm still suspended."

"So tell me about the meeting," Neil says. "Who was present, what impact do those people have on your job at the school, and how do you usually feel about those people?"

My upper lip curls and my brows raise. I take a deep breath.

"Okay, well, there was Principal Gwen Miller, and the HR coordinator Tanner Pike. The principal is technically my boss on paper, but Tanner struts around like he owns the place and she lets him. Tanner seems to be proud of catching employees breaking policy. Miller is an okay principal, I guess. But she's clueless about what it's like to be in my role day to day. Plus she never sticks up for me when it matters."

Tension spreads through my chest as I continue. "Then the school district superintendent Ragsdale was there. It's reelection season, so he's greasing the wheels. After he's reelected we won't see him again for a year unless some scandal breaks out. He's gunning for the state super position, so nothing else matters."

As usual, Kendra is busily recording what I say.

Neil nods. "Okay, so describe the meeting, your part in it; did anyone get heated? Was any part of it unpleasant or uncomfortable?"

I blow out a breath. "Yeah, I'd say the entire thing was unpleasant and uncomfortable. Principal Miller wanted more details about how much time I spend in each one-on-one meeting with a kid. But she lets Tanner Pike answer, because apparently they were keeping a clock. According to them, I spend too much time when I'm one-on-one. It's been a constant challenge. They wanted to know, if my suspension is overturned, what my plan was for improving my numbers. What they meant was, when am I going to cut the time I spend with one kid so I can have more appointments during the day. Apparently the numbers they've established look better for funding. Everyone in administration knows they need to hire a second school counselor, but they've made it clear that's not going to happen. On top of that, the month before my suspension they decided to take a look at my job description because Ragsdale has some pet data reporting project that nobody else wants to do, and I had no choice but to take it on. No extra compensation. No consideration for the load already on my plate. He just dumped it on me."

My chest tightens even more and my breathing rate increases as anger creeps in.

"And now, they've put me on a suspension with only partial pay because of my involvement in the Aimee Dixon case. Apparently I broke policy because I didn't ask permission, which was completely unintentional. But intentions don't matter at all, I guess." Rubbing my eyes with the palms of my hands, I will the mounting pressure to dissipate. It doesn't work. My fists clench and unclench.

"They don't get it!" I bark. "They have no idea what some of these kids are going through, and for some of them I'm the only person they have ever talked to who will actually listen to them and believe them. I can't put a timer on a kid who's crying because her mom moved another deadbeat alcoholic boyfriend into the house and now she has to hide in her little sister's room and cover her sister's ears so her sister doesn't hear them fighting every night. Miller wants me to give that girl exactly fourteen minutes on a stopwatch and then send her back to class. Ragsdale is absolutely not there for those kids. I don't even know how the guy ended up in education. Reminds me of my own high school principal; he absolutely hated kids."

Sudden sleepiness threatens to overwhelm me.

Neil is writing as he asks, "So how threatened do you remember feeling at that point in the meeting on Monday?"

Before Neil can finish his question, I see Garrison begin to stride toward me. Leaning back and crossing my arms, I drift into a quiet, mindless void.

22

AGE FORTY-NINE

The gentle sound of my wife's voice floats into my consciousness. *Why am I sitting up?* I hear another man's voice. *Who is that?*

Opening my eyes with a deep breath, I finally reorient. *Ugh.* I'm still at the shrink's office. A glance at my watch shows almost forty minutes have passed.

"Are you with us, Danny?" Neil asks.

I look between him and Grace. Kendra is right where I last saw her, and now Garrison stands beside her at ease. "Did I check out again?" I ask.

Grace puts a reassuring hand on my knee. She doesn't seem frustrated or sad like she usually is when I check out. She seems energized. "You did, sweetie. But some very interesting things happened while you were gone. Do you want to hear them?"

Do I? This is so bizarre. "Sure. I guess."

"Danny," Neil begins. "Earlier I mentioned that it sounds

like you're dissociating, and based on the last forty minutes, I am certain of it."

"Why?" Red heat creeps up my neck onto my cheeks. "What'd I do?"

Neil looks at Grace. It's clear he wants her to explain.

Grace pivots to face me fully. "So, when Neil asked if you felt threatened in the staff meeting, you sat back and kind of checked out for a second. But then your face changed a little bit. You started acting annoyed, like your leg started bouncing, you started biting your nails, and you kept shaking your head and running your fingers through your hair. You definitely weren't acting like yourself."

I look to Neil and back to Grace. *No way.*

"Then Neil asked you what your name was, and in a kind of squeaky, high-pitched voice, you said that your name was Jeremy."

My brows furrow. "Why would I call myself that? My name isn't Jeremy. My name is Danny."

Neil clears his throat. "So in the world of dissociation, a personality that identifies itself by another name with different personality characteristics from the primary person, we call that an alter. Like an alternative."

I had read a little about this studying for my masters. I always thought it was something people made up to get attention, or maybe it really came from a brain tumor. "How do you know I wasn't just sleepwalking or having a nightmare?" I ask.

"You definitely weren't asleep, Danny," he answers. "This alter, this Jeremy, talked to us for over half an hour."

Garrison and Kendra exchange worried glances.

I am definitely crazy.

"So what'd you all talk about?" I try to joke.

Neil slides a legal pad across his desk to Grace for her to pick up.

She gathers her thoughts for a moment. "So, when Jeremy told Neil what his name was, Neil asked him how old he was, and if he had a particular job in your mind. So he said he is fourteen, and he calls himself the gatekeeper."

I scoff. "What, like I'm a kid in his mom's basement playing in a video game kind of gatekeeper?"

Neil answers. "In dissociation, the alter known as the gatekeeper has access to every traumatic memory that the primary person, called the core, has ever experienced. So this role of the gatekeeper is to control what personality comes up at what time. They can be any age, any gender, any nationality, even any religion."

Grace continues. "So Neil asked Jeremy if there was anything he wanted us to know, and he said that the others were tired of not being acknowledged, so he wanted to make sure everyone had their facts straight."

My heart pounds. "What do you mean, 'the Others?'" I dare not look toward Kendra or Garrison.

Grace moves the legal pad so I can see it. "Look, Danny. Jeremy wrote down absolutely everything." She looks at Neil. "What did you call this? The structure?"

"The system," Neil answers. "That's the technical word for it."

I run my hand over the words written on the page. Normally my handwriting is professional and polished. It looks nothing like the juvenile writing I see here.

"You're saying I wrote this?" I ask.

"Technically, no," Neil says. "You didn't write that. The

alter personality that took over who calls himself Jeremy wrote it."

Grace points to the page. "Danny, do any of these things make sense to you? Look at the names and the roles they have taken."

Like reading a cast list on the playbill at a live musical theater, my finger skims down the list of names with their ages and the role they apparently play in this system inside my head as Neil calls it.

I freeze about one-third of the way down the list.

Garrison. Age 30. Soldier and protector.

Garrison's combat boots are visible in my peripheral vision, but I can't look at him. My finger slides down to the next name.

Kendra. Age 47. Scribe and reporter.

Glancing from Kendra to Grace to Neil and back to the page, I cough nervously.

A few more lines down. *The Bossman. Age 25. Encourager and big brother. Tiny Tot. Age 4. The one allowed to cry.*

Grace leans in at my discomfort. "What's going on in your head, babe?"

Squeezing my eyes shut, I pinch the bridge of my nose. "So, Neil. Tell me. All these alters or people or whatever you call them. Do people ever see them as if they're actually there? You know, like *A Beautiful Mind* crazytown seeing people that don't really exist, but to them, they're real, only no one else sees them?"

"I'd never use the word 'crazytown,' Danny. But yes. You yourself have said many times that crazy has a name. A lot of times, that name is actually trauma. The mind is a complex piece of machinery. And when trauma happens, especially repeated trauma at an early age, the mind can fracture in all kinds of ways. So yes, sometimes some people do see some of these alters, perhaps pretty regularly."

So I am certifiably crazy.

"Danny, let me in," Grace begs gently. "You reacted to a name on this list. Which one is it?"

I blow out a deep breath and point to Kendra's name first. "This one, here. This Kendra. She's standing right over Neil's left shoulder."

Both Neil and Grace look toward where I indicate, but I know they don't see her.

"She's got her hair up in a bun. She's wearing horn-rimmed glasses, she's holding a clipboard, and she writes down everything I say, all the time. If I'm awake, she's there. She's been there my whole life."

Grace and Neil are silent. Then I point to another name on the list. "And this one. Garrison. He's standing just to Kendra's left in the same corner." I point but I don't look at him. "He wears army fatigues and combat boots, and he stands at attention. He's not visible one hundred percent of the time like Kendra is. But he's around a lot, especially if I'm in an uncomfortable situation."

Grace leans in. "Anyone else?"

She believes me.

I point to the Bossman. "I know this one's name. I never see him. I just hear him inside my head. Usually he's annoyed with me, and he's always telling me I'm fine and to stop acting like a baby. He's not very nice. Then there's Brody. He's the punk fighter. He's like a one-man justice league. And I know Tiny Tot. He's the little one who's allowed to cry."

The remaining names on the list are unfamiliar, but I count them up.

Ten pieces. Me and nine friends.

I fight tears that threaten to break as heat rises up my neck. Part of me is relieved and moved that Gracie believes me. The rest of me is deeply ashamed and embarrassed by what we've all just learned.

"Why would God do something like this to me, Neil?" I ask, anger blooming. "I mean, if 'God is love' and all that, why would He make me just as crazy as my mother if He's supposed to be love? I just don't get it."

Neil opens his palms toward me. "If I had the answer to that, I'd be a rich man."

His watch beeps softly. "Okay, Danny. So, thankfully we are at a point of actual diagnosis. This is a clear case of Dissociative Identity Disorder, which I'm sure you know they used to call Multiple Personality Disorder. This diagnosis is a good thing, because now we can move forward with starting a more appropriate therapy. There's a ton of breakthrough techniques and new research that will make a huge difference in how we proceed after today."

A tiny glimmer of hope flickers in my chest as I rise to shake Neil's hand.

"Thanks, man," I say as we walk toward the door. "So, how long are we talking?"

"What do you mean?"

"To be cured. From this dissociating. How long does that normally take once we start working on it specifically?"

Neil draws a full breath as he looks at me with sadness. My flicker extinguishes in an instant.

"Danny, there is no cure."

23

AGE FORTY-NINE

"Don't trust these people," warns the Bossman. "They're probably judgy and hypocritical just like all the other church people have always been. Don't you dare let your guard down."

"I know, I know," I mutter under my breath as Grace and I walk down the sanctuary aisle to find a seat.

Living Waters Chapel looks different from any other church I've been to. Usually I would expect a raised, carpeted platform with an ornate lectern and several velvet-covered pulpit chairs and a robed choir in the loft behind. I would also expect long, padded wooden pews with hardback hymnals placed at every third seat. This place has none of those things.

A small worship band plays softly, the musicians seated on bar stools across a low, plain stage. A simple metal podium stands front and center on the floor, and massive media screens flank the room. Comfortable, thickly padded chairs are arranged in semi-circle rows on a polished concrete floor. Chatty laughter fills the room as people mingle and sip coffee while children dodge and weave through the aisles. The positive energy is palpable. This feels more like my school auditorium on PTA night than a church.

I like it.

"Grace! Danny!" A woman's voice calls out from several rows over. Looking across the growing crowd, I see a short, gray-haired woman smiling and waving. Grace grabs my hand and tugs.

"That's my new friend Claudia! She's the lady I've been telling you about from the women's Bible study."

"Remember what I said, Danny," says the Bossman.

"Yeah, yeah, I heard you," I whisper. As we move closer to Grace's friend, Kendra steps up behind her.

Claudia pulls Grace in for a hug. "Oh, I'm so glad you both made it!" She extends a hand to me. "Hi, Danny. I'm Claudia Fowler, and this is my husband, Jim."

The bald, wiry man seated next to her stands and gives me a firm handshake. "Jim Fowler," he says with a nod and a kind smile.

"Danny," I nod back. "Danny Pierce. I'm Grace's husband. Nice to meet you."

We all take a seat. "So, Danny, what do you do?" asks Jim.

"Well, I'm a high school counselor, but I'm kind of on a break at the moment."

No need to explain that I'm crazy and got myself fired.

Jim's face brightens. "Wow, what a calling! I just love being around teenagers. They're authentic, you know? They see things as they genuinely are, and they don't hold back. It's so refreshing. And when they get lit up for Jesus, man, look out!"

I laugh. "Yeah, they're brutally honest, you got that right. How 'bout you? What do you do?"

He straightens. "Retired army major out of Fort Bragg. Loved it and hated it. But mostly loved it."

"I can definitely identify with that!"

I smile at Grace and Claudia as they chatter and giggle like girls. My wife clearly enjoys the connection with this woman.

"We don't like this couple," says the Bossman. "They're dangerous, and you need to stay away from them. Take everything they say with a huge grain of salt. Don't be sucked in."

"Getting a little bit paranoid are we?" I ask with a snicker.

"I mean it, Danny, these people will try to get you to believe things that are not true. Don't fall for it."

I sigh. "Noted."

A bearded hipster in skinny jeans addresses the crowd from the podium as the worship team turns up the volume. "Welcome to Living Waters! I'm Pastor Glen, and I'm so glad you're all here on this beautifully rainy spring day. We especially want to welcome any visitors and guests; we bless you and pray that you have an encounter with the Lord today. Lord Jesus, we welcome You into this place and proclaim You as Lord of all. Father God, we praise and thank You for Your unconditional love and for the incredible gift of salvation. Holy Spirit, You are welcome here. Come and have Your way. I ask this in the mighty name of Jesus, amen. Would you stand with me as we worship the Lord?"

For a solid forty-five minutes I am awash in worship like I've never heard or seen. The worship band doesn't draw attention to themselves through choreographed stage movements or dramatic orchestration. Every one of them plays and sings with their eyes closed, unconcerned about the rest of us in the room. They also sing directly *to* Jesus; they're not just singing *about* Him. At times it's so intimate that I feel as if I'm eavesdropping on a private conversation.

A few times I am unexpectedly moved to tears at the words of the worship. It never crossed my mind to tell Jesus directly that I loved Him. This concept fills me with confusion and wonder.

The worship team also sings phrases about love that pours from the eyes of Jesus. The concept of looking at Jesus face-to-face melts my heart and terrifies me at the same time. My heart is stirred as I consider a Savior who would actually want to be with me as a person.

Pastor Glen's message doesn't feel anything like a sermon. He engages in conversational dialogue with the congregation, just like a group of friends having a discussion. Today he talks about the Biblical account of the woman with the issue of blood who reached out to grab the corner of Jesus' garment. My mind reels at the revelation that the Jewish prayer tassels hanging on the corner of the Lord's garment were actually referred to in the Old Testament as a source of healing. I'm mesmerized at how this changes the story.

Pastor Glen and a group that he calls his prayer team also spend time praying at the end of the service in a way I've never seen before. Quite a few people move toward the front, and two-person teams place their hands on the head or shoulders of the one they are praying for. This isn't the altar call for salvation like I've seen many Sundays at other churches, riddled with guilt and condemnation. This is an invitation for something much more personal and specific.

As soon as the service ends, we all stand to make our way

out. Jim grabs my hand and claps me on the back. "Let us take you all out to lunch! Our treat. There's a great Mexican place just around the corner. Sound good?"

Before I can protest, Grace answers, "That sounds fabulous, we would love to. I just need to grab the kids."

The Bossman snaps. "This doesn't sound like staying away from these people, Danny! Didn't you hear me say that they're dangerous? What are you doing?!"

My brows furrow at his level of agitation. "Geez man, chill out would you?" I say under my breath. "I'm not getting any axe murderer vibes from these people so back off. It's just lunch."

If it's just lunch, why am I so sweaty?

The meal is unexpectedly enjoyable, and the food is delicious as promised. Jim and Claudia interact with Josiah and Abigail with the tender ease of seasoned grandparents. My kids are enamored with the intentional conversation and genuine interest. The Fowlers are both very easy to like, even more so when Claudia presents a handful of quarters for the kids to go spend in the arcade crane game machine.

As the kids play nearby while we wait for dessert, Jim clasps his hands under his chin, elbows on the table. "Okay if I tell you a personal story, Danny?"

"Sure," I say, ignoring Kendra as she stands behind Jim and starts to write.

Jim clears his throat and pauses for a moment. "I have a younger sister. Her name is Sandra. I was two years old when she was born. We were best buddies when we were little. But for some reason I'll never understand, my mama never liked Sandra. Never wanted her, never said she loved her. It was pretty obvious that I was the golden child. Then when I was about five, my mama and daddy split up. It was horrible. They both drank a lot, and they'd try to kill each other when they got hammered."

Sounds familiar.

"I guess both of them were cheating on each other. Neither one of them knew the Lord, so there was no trying to save the marriage. But when they got divorced and my daddy moved out, my mother started bringing men over to the house. Cruel men."

Not sure I like where this is going.

Jim takes a long swig of iced tea followed by a deep breath. "Sandra was only three years old. And some of those bad men, they liked to hurt little girls. None of them ever laid a hand on me. But they hurt Sandra real bad. Worst part is, Mama looked the other way. She never once bothered to ask about the marks or the bruises on her own daughter. I think in some sick way, Mama was jealous of Sandra. I tried to get in between her and one of those guys when I was about nine. He beat me to a pulp and said if I ever did that again, he'd kill my whole family. Mama stood off to the side and witnessed the whole thing. Then we all went on as if nothing had ever happened."

I glance at Grace. Her lack of surprise tells me she's heard the story before. The pain in my heart takes my breath away.

Why do I feel like this is a setup?

"So when we were teenagers, I guess maybe I was sixteen, so she'd be about thirteen, I started noticing that sometimes Sandra would be a completely different person. Like normally she was reserved and shy, as you can imagine after living through all of that trauma. But then one day I get home from school, and she's chatty and bouncing around the house without a care in the world. She had makeup on, she'd fixed her hair. She'd cleaned her room up, which she normally flat out refused to do. So I start asking her questions, trying to understand what's going on. Then she tells me her name is Robin, and that Sandra went away for a little while."

"See, Danny?" urges the Bossman. "I TOLD YOU. These people are NOT safe. You need to leave. NOW."

Wait a minute. They know?!

Face flushed, I look between Grace and Jim. "You told them? You told complete strangers?" White hot pain shoots through my heart as Kendra scowls and writes faster.

Reaching across the table to place a hand on mine, Grace gazes into my eyes with love. "Sweetheart, these people understand what we're going through because they've lived it firsthand. I didn't volunteer your story. Claudia shared Sandra's story with the women's Bible study, and she offered to pray for people who were struggling with the same thing."

Brody and Tiny Tot come to stand on either side of me. Unsure if I'll need them or not, I let them stay. I close my eyes.

I want to crawl in a hole and die.

Claudia's gentle voice breaks in. "Danny, I know how overwhelming this must feel for you right now. That's to be expected. But I also need you to hear me. Son, will you look at me?"

Chin raised, I peek at Claudia.

"Your story is completely safe here, and we hold absolutely zero judgment of you. What happened to your mind is because of the trauma you went through. I've only heard just a fraction of the story from Grace, but the little I do know is absolutely tragic."

Defenses lowering, my shoulders slump. "That's a good word for it."

"Can I tell you the rest of the story?" Jim asks. The kindness in his eyes breaks through my unease.

I shrug. "May as well, I guess."

"So by the time I went away to basic training, Sandra's mind had split into at least four alternate personalities. I already mentioned Robin, she was the bouncy, carefree, hyper-positive one who cared about making friends and being popular. Then there was Polly. She was the raging fighter. I cannot count the number of people she left with a black eye. There was Tiffany. She acted like she was five or six years old and wanted to play with dolls. And then there was Crystal. She was the one who found drugs and alcohol."

Mouth agape, my brows raise.

Someone who understands me!

Jim continues. "Mama never figured it out. Sandra was unpredictable, so that just made Mama even madder. She kicked Sandra out of the house a few times; Mama lied to the police and accused her of stealing when she hadn't. It was awful."

Heaviness lingers over the table.

I break the silence. "So, what happened?"

A flash of sadness crosses Jim's face. "Over time, the personality that went by Crystal seemed to become dominant. That was over the course of maybe eight years, I guess. Eventually I stopped hearing from Sandra completely. And of course, Crystal fell into full blown addiction. Meth, cocaine, acid, heroin. Whatever she could find. And then there was all the behavior that comes along with that lifestyle. Prostitution, petty theft. She's got a rap sheet a mile long. She borrowed or stole thousands of dollars from us and never paid back a penny. We finally had to stop giving her money."

The restaurant server plops down a large platter of cinnamon churros and caramel dip. Grace and Claudia help themselves.

"So the weekend of her thirty-fifth birthday, she got into some bad dope. They think maybe it was laced with something or maybe she OD'd. Forensics back in the day were nothing like they are today. But whatever was in there totally fried her brain. She had a couple of strokes, and she became an invalid. She couldn't talk, couldn't walk. She had to wear a diaper."

Jim pauses to wipe a tear from his eye.

Claudia continues the story. "So Jim's mother had already passed away, and Sandra didn't have any family. We prayed at length about it, we sought wise counsel, and we had honest conversations with the whole family. We felt strongly that the Lord was inviting us to bring Sandra into our home and provide care for her. So that's what we did."

"Wow," I answer. "I don't know many people who would do that. I doubt I could."

Claudia smiles. "We heard that from a lot of people. Some of our friends told us we were insane. But we just had a beautiful peace about it. I won't pretend it wasn't hard. We still had teenagers at home, Jim was still working. Sandra required a ton of specialized care. But Jesus was with us every moment. He gave both of us a supernatural love and compassion for Sandra that neither one of us could have mustered up on our own."

Quarters spent and cheap toys in hand, Josiah and Abigail crash back into their seats and dive into dessert.

Jim chimes back in. "It was fascinating to see how she started to respond to us. The first year was really rough. She was combative, she couldn't relax. I think the part of her brain that survived was just mad at the whole world. But we talked to her and prayed aloud over her every single day. We'd play Christian music, we'd anoint her head with oil and lay our hands on her head and invite the presence of the Lord to come. And we would tell her how loved she was, that in scripture it says she was the apple of her Father God's eye, that she was fearfully and wonderfully made. After several months of doing that, we noticed a big shift. She was calmer, she wouldn't fight the nurses. Her face would brighten when we'd come into the room. It was apparent that there was a part inside of her that understood."

It's Grace's turn to wipe away a tear. "That's incredible," she whispers.

Claudia nods. "It was miraculous. And we had about two years of that, where Sandra was responsive and peaceful. But sadly she'd done a real number on her organs from all the drugs. She went downhill really fast; I think from the first signs of organ failure until she eventually died was less than three weeks. But she passed away surrounded by people who loved her. And we literally felt the presence of Jesus come into the room as she took her last breath."

"Wow," I whisper.

"Danny," says Jim. "We considered it an honor to love on Sandra despite everything. The person Sandra was to the rest of the world, the crackhead, the nut job with five names, the thief. Those things weren't her identity. That's not who the Lord designed her to be. So we made the choice to see her as Jesus did. So I know it's probably upsetting that Grace shared a little bit of your story with us. But we understand that all the things you've been to the rest of the world, those things aren't who the Lord designed you to be."

Claudia pats the top of my hand. "We're not here to fix you, or judge you, or even tell you what you should do. We certainly don't have all the answers. We just want you to know that we're here for you, for both of you, in complete and total confidence. And we'll be praying for you. We have no agenda. We're just trying to be Jesus with skin on."

It's my turn to wipe away a lone tear.

I have never felt as known as I am right now.

Garrison, Kendra, Brody, and Tiny Tot stand huddled together in the corner behind Claudia in a heated conversation. They all stop and glare at me with a scowl, arms crossed.

I look back between Claudia and Jim, peace and love emanating from them both.

Wow, this feels new. I'm not afraid of these people.

24

AGE FORTY-NINE

I am staring at life where death should be.

I buckle at the knees again as the weight of reality hits me.

Abigail, my youngest, finally sleeps. Her four-year-old frame appears tiny against the heavy hospital bed, made even smaller by the oversized blood pressure cuff and the skidproof yellow hospital footies that hang over the ends of her feet. My wife sleeps in the cot right next to her, one arm reaching through the bedrails to hold Abigail's hand. There's not a shred of evidence of this morning's trauma visible anywhere on her peaceful little face. Reaching over both of them, I gently move a wisp of Abigail's hair away from her face as I wonder how I deserve the blessing of children.

This morning had started off like any other summer Tuesday while I'm still on eternal administrative suspension. School systems take forever with these things.

Grace and the kids had headed out to her sister's house

with plans to hang out by the neighborhood swimming pool all day while I caught up on balancing the bank accounts. A brief flurry of cereal-flavored kisses and "I love you's" and they left me to a quiet office. About ninety minutes later, as I was just starting my second cup of coffee, my cell phone rang. My favorite picture of Grace popped up on the caller ID.

I pressed the speakerphone button to answer, and I could hear screaming and a siren in the background.

"Grace, what's going on?!" A lump shot up into my throat. "Are you okay?"

Her voice pierced my very soul. "Danny! Abigail drowned! She's dead! Oh my God, Danny, she's all blue! My baby is dead! Jesus, noooooo! Don't take my baby! Noooooo!!"

A surreal peace washed over me as I stood to find my keys.

"Where are they taking her?" I asked, assertive but calm. "I'm leaving right now."

Grace hadn't heard me over her conversation with her sister nearby. "Sarah, get your church to start praying," I heard Grace order. "Take Josiah back to your house with your kids, and all of you start praying and don't stop."

She brought the phone back to her ear. "Danny, I don't know what happened. I'm so sorry! I was putting sunscreen on Josiah, and I turned around and she was floating."

I could barely understand her from the anguish and panic in her voice.

"Where is she now?" I asked as I climbed into my car and fastened the seatbelt.

"The paramedics are doing CPR on her. She's up on a

gurney and they're wheeling her into an ambulance. Danny, she's all blue and puffy! Jesus, no!"

The phone connection switched over to the Bluetooth speaker in my car. "Listen to me, Grace. Get in the ambulance with her. Don't take no for an answer. I'll meet you, I just need to know where."

A stabbing pain cut through my heart as I recognized the sound of my oldest crying as he screamed Abigail's name. Through all of the chatter and shuffling on the other end of the line, I finally heard a male voice explain to Grace that they were headed to Children's Hospital South Lexington. Ignoring the blaring horns around me, I whipped my car into a U-turn in the middle of the street and floored the gas.

The Bossman spoke up. "Just breathe, Danny. You've got this, no matter what happens."

"SHUT UP!" I shouted. "You don't get to talk to me right now!"

Cognitively dissociating from the trauma I was hearing over the phone, I breathed slowly and deeply as I sped my way around side streets and turning lanes to make it onto the interstate. As I accelerated through the on-ramp, Grace finally came back to the phone.

"Okay, I'm in the ambulance with her. They're still working on her. Abigail! Wake up, baby! Jesus, come wake up this baby!"

I knew my wife's faith was deep and strong. I didn't realize that her faith could actually expect a miracle like this. We had already been on the phone for over fifteen minutes.

"Danny," she said, fighting the trembling in her voice. "I'm gonna call the ladies in my Bible study. I need you to call Pastor Glen, call Claudia Fowler, and anyone else who can pray for Abigail. I mean absolutely everyone. And you pray, too. I'll meet you at the hospital. I love you."

The Bluetooth beeped as the line went dead, and the radio came on, programmed to the Christian channel that Grace liked. I didn't recognize the song that started to play, something about raising a hallelujah in a storm. *Yeah, right, like that makes sense.*

At first I balked at Grace's request to rally people for prayer. Would they think we're like the religious fanatics who ask everyone to pray all the time? Deciding it couldn't hurt and knowing it would make Grace feel better, I called.

My thumb tapped the speakerphone icon on the steering wheel. I spoke aloud after the system prompt. "Call Pastor Glen."

He answered on the first ring. "Danny Pierce! Great to hear from you, man!"

"Listen, Pastor, there's been an accident. My youngest daughter Abigail is being taken to Children's South. Grace said she drowned in the pool and they're working on her. Grace wanted me to call and ask you to pray." My monotone voice carried zero emotion.

"Dear Jesus in heaven," he whispered. "Absolutely. Of course. I'll call everyone on the church leadership team, and we'll activate the prayer chain and our team of intercessors. Have faith, Danny. I've seen God do bigger miracles than this!"

I hung up without saying goodbye. Bigger than this? What could that possibly mean? Grace said Abigail was already blue and puffy.

Repeating the same stoic conversation with the three other

names I knew were in my phone contacts, I raced down the highway. I was still twenty minutes from the hospital. I tried to call Grace again but it went straight to voicemail.

The background noise of the car radio drifted back into my consciousness. As the words of the song played softly, my protective wall of stoicism began to crumble. The artist on the radio was singing a phrase that Pastor Glen had just preached about last Sunday at church.

"Be still, and know that I am God."

Garrison stared at me with Tiny Tot sitting in his lap. I didn't acknowledge them, and they both turned to face forward and stare straight ahead.

Speeding down the interstate, I looked toward the clouds. Fighting back an eruption of panic, I started talking out loud.

"Okay, God. I know that You and I haven't been on the best of terms. And we both know how much I have screwed– uh, sorry–messed up. But God, don't punish Abigail because of me. She doesn't deserve that, God. She deserves a long, happy life. I don't deserve one. But she does."

I wiped at the tears starting down my face.

"God, I don't know about all of this raising from the dead faith stuff. I know You saved me back when I was a punk. But Pastor Glen said he's seen You do bigger things. And now I hear this song playing like You're talking to me. Maybe I'm just crazy. I don't know. But God, whatever You want from me, whatever it takes, if You'll just save my baby girl…"

My voice cracked as my throat closed up at the weight of the situation we were in. My shoulders heaved as I fought hard to regain control of my emotions.

"God, I will do anything. You know where my faith is, and You know that Grace has a thousand times more faith than I do. So God, if You won't do it for me, I ask You to do this for her."

A new awareness of the pain my wife must have been feeling washed over me, and heaving sobs began to erupt. "Please, God! I'm begging You. If there is any goodness and mercy in You, would You please save our baby girl?! Please God!"

Swimming in panic, I couldn't think of anything else to say other than to repeat the phrase "please, God" over and over. Even as I parked the car and ran into the emergency entrance, my lips continued to plead with the same phrase.

Pushing past the line of people waiting to be seen, I tapped hard on the counter in front of a nurse. The volume of my voice left no room for negotiation.

"My four-year-old daughter, Abigail Pierce, she was just brought in by ambulance from a drowning accident."

Another nurse stepped forward behind the counter. "Danny Pierce?" she asked.

"Yes, yes that's me."

She pointed to a set of blue double doors across the room. "Meet me at the blue entrance."

The doors were already opening by the time I crossed the room. The nurse was waiting for me on the other side of the doors, and the solemn look on her face sent a new wave of dread over me.

"Have they told you anything?" I asked. "What are they doing? I need to know what's going on."

She didn't look at me as we walked quickly through a maze of hallways. "I don't have any new information, Mr. Pierce. I know that they were doing everything they could."

Rounding a corner, we came into a section of glass-walled

rooms brimming with people. I saw Grace looking through one of the windows with her hands and her forehead pressed against the glass.

I fought the collapse of my own knees as I called out Grace's name. As I opened my arms to her, she crumpled into me. I held her heaving frame with her face buried into my chest, and noticed Garrison as he walked up beside us. I stared into the room where Abigail was.

There must have been a dozen people all clustered around the bed. Between their elbows and medical scrubs, I caught a quick glimpse of Abigail's little feet.

They definitely didn't look blue to me.

My mouth was stuck muttering "please God" over and over as I watched. Then I saw a couple of nurses jump back quickly away from one side of the bed as water hit the floor and splattered everywhere. A collective cheer with applause immediately followed.

"Gracie, look," I whispered into my wife's ear as I turned her around to face the glass. We both heard the most beautiful sound.

Abigail was coughing and yelling "Mommy!" at the same time.

My baby girl was alive.

Grace barreled into the room as I found myself unable to stand. Crawling slowly in an aimless circle on the floor, I sobbed as deep waves of gratitude flooded over me. I could do nothing for several minutes but crawl and weep as I muttered, "Thank You, God. Thank You, God. Thank You, God."

Now as I watch Grace and Abigail rest, I play the day over and over in my mind. I rehash less about all of the medical trauma, and more about what Abigail told us just before she drifted off to sleep.

Grace had crawled into the hospital bed beside Abigail and they were both coloring quietly together. Grace started the conversation as they colored.

"So, baby girl, do you remember what happened today?"

Abigail's eyes never left her coloring page. "You mean when I was under the water in the pool?"

"Mmm-hmm," Grace answered.

"Well, it was super quiet. I don't know how I ended up down there. I tried to call you, but you couldn't hear me under the water."

Gracie's eyes glistened as she answered. "I know, sweet girl, and Mommy is so, so sorry she didn't hear you."

Abigail exchanged her crayon for a new color and continued. "I wasn't scared though. I had a friend with me."

Grace and I exchanged a quick glance.

"Oh, yeah?" I asked, moving to sit on the end of the bed. "Who was the friend? Do you know her name?"

"It's not a 'her,' Daddy. It was Jesus. I've seen Him before in the pictures at church. He has a beard like Papa, but it's brown. And He told me not to be scared, and that He was taking me back to you and Mommy."

My mouth dropped open, but I couldn't speak.

"Then there was all this glittery, bright stuff around Him, and then I fell asleep, and then I woke up here."

Grace had stopped coloring and held her crayon in midair. Tears fell as she could barely speak. "You... you saw Jesus?"

Abigail nodded. "Yep. He was nice. His shirt was pretty, too. It was glowing bright, and He had a long blue scarf hanging over one of His shoulders, and the rest of His scarf was around His tummy. I'm hungry, Mommy. Can I have a snack?"

Kissing the side of Abigail's head, Grace wiped more tears away as she slid out of the bed to go find a snack.

Jesus Himself had saved my baby girl.

25

AGE FORTY-NINE

My real mother truly loves me, and I know I'll see her in heaven with Jesus.

Sweaty and flecked with dirt, I sit on the back porch steps and clutch the letter I've just read six times. I weep openly in an unfamiliar mixture of gratitude and grief, wondering why Tiny Tot isn't here to cry for me. It's strange, feeling my own emotions. But I welcome it.

With all of my free time since being suspended from work, thankfully with partial pay, I've been taking advantage of the opportunity to catch up on the never-ending "to-do" list around the house. This morning as Grace had driven off to her new part-time job, I was already dragging the ladder to the back corner of the house where the gutters had begun to sprout their own forest.

Remarkably, neither Abigail nor Josiah seemed to carry any sort of trauma or anxiety from Abigail's accident several weeks ago. Grace's parents had already picked them up this morning for a play day. So until Grace and the kids got home midafternoon, it was just me and my tools.

Isolation can be a friend. Or a foe. Or both at the same time. The Others sometimes bombarded my thoughts the most when things were quiet. Today I decided not to play that game, so as I worked in the rising July heat, I busied my mind thinking about Abigail's story of meeting Jesus.

Wireless earbuds in, I found a Christian music playlist. Every single song seemed to speak directly to me, either about God hearing my desperate prayer, or about Jesus coming through with nothing other than an absolute miracle. I hadn't given much thought to Christian music before, other than Sunday mornings at church. Today it spoke more than I ever thought possible.

Gutters cleaned and debris blown away, I hung the ladder back on its pegs in the tool shed as a song about gratitude began to play through my earbuds. Pausing to take in the cloudless summer sky and the crepe myrtle trees in full bloom, I allowed myself to remember the gratefulness that had poured out of me when Abigail started breathing again. Chin tilted skyward, sweaty and dirty from cleaning the gutters, I closed my eyes and breathed deeply.

"God," I said aloud, "I know I said it a lot that day, but thank You. A million times, thank You."

A tender thought floated in. "There's a beautiful destiny planned for her, Danny."

"Destiny? What do you mean, like fate?"

A gentle laugh blended with His answer. "No, not like the world uses that word today. I mean the plans I've had for her from the beginning."

I nodded as the words from the Bible verse about good plans in the book of Jeremiah rolled through my mind.

For I know the plans I have for you, declares the LORD, plans to prosper you and not to harm you, plans to give you hope and a future.

"You have your own beautiful destiny too, son."

I dropped my head. "A destiny to be mentally insane? Doesn't sound very much like prospering for hope and a future to me."

His response was tender and patient. "You have so much to learn, Danny."

My answer was interrupted by the squealing of hydraulic brakes coming from the front of the house. Slipping off my gloves and turning off my earbuds, I made my way around to the front of the house where a delivery truck sat in my driveway. A tall, wiry man in a brown uniform hopped down from his seat and trotted my direction.

"Delivery for Danny Pierce?" he asked, presenting a large envelope to me.

"That's me, man. Thanks." I signed his digital clipboard and flipped the envelope around as I headed to the backyard again. My eyes fell on the sender's address.

Sunset Ridge. Franklin, TN.

Gypsy's letter.

Time slowed as I fumbled to carefully open the envelope in the late morning breeze. Finally getting the package opened, I took a deep breath as I reached in and pulled out a small stack of lined notebook paper folded in half. As I sat on the back porch steps, Garrison and Kendra came walking toward me.

177

I waved them away with my hand. "I'm good here. Don't need you right now."

Twisting my neck from side to side to get a good crack, I breathed deeply again and unfolded the pages. A grainy, wallet-sized photo of a little boy fell from the pages.

Dear Danny,

I think that's what they call you. If you got this letter, it means I ain't on the earth no more. I already got things took care of, so you don't gotta worry about nothing.

The first thing I wanna say is I love you. I'm sure that's real hard to believe since I was only your mom for about four years and didn't see you but a few times after that. I know I was pretty messed up. But I thought about you and missed you every single day of my life since they took you away. Inside here is the last picture I had of you. Kept it with me every-where. Sorry for the stain on the back.

Running my thumb over the little photo, I saw inno-cence and spunk in the happy little kid's face looking back at me. I chuckle at the 1970s Sesame Street T-shirt I'm wearing.

I also wanna tell you I found Jesus, and He made real big changes in my life. One of the nurses at Sunset Ridge knows Jesus. Her name is Viola, and she started praying for me soon as I got here. She wasn't all religious like the other church people I've known. She talked about Jesus like He was her best friend, and she prayed like nobody I ever heard before. Whenever she was around, I had fewer episodes and I just felt peaceful. She found me a Bible and taught me how to read it where it made sense, and I was getting it.

Viola also showed me about forgiveness. I fought that for a long time. I think I told you the bad things I went through as a kid, so you can imagine how hard a time I had forgiving. Viola was so patient with me. But I get it now. I wish I woulda met Viola a long time ago!

You probably figured out that I see and hear people who ain't really there. At least, nobody else sees them, but I do. Some doctors called it a personality disorder. I finally learned after trying everything for years that my mind is broke. I tried every medicine they gave me, but it either made it worse or turned me into a zombie. I didn't always do the right thing either. People say I got a stubborn streak! But since I found Jesus, the other people I see and hear in my head just don't matter as much anymore. Some days are still better than others. But it's been so quiet in my head when I play worship songs, or read my Bible (especially the Psalms), or when Viola prays with me.

I'm so sorry things happened the way they did. When they took you and Danielle away from me after *all I was doing to make our lives better, I went crazier than I ever did before. I got in so much trouble that no lawyer would ever try to help me find you or get you back. I was too messed up to be a good mom for you and your sister. I hated myself for years over all of it. Your birthdays and Christmas were always so hard, and I usually had to get high to make the pain go away. That never worked anyway. With Jesus I finally forgave myself. Now I don't gotta get high on you and your sister's birthdays lately. Instead I use those days to pray for both of you, praying that you're safe and doing real good, and that you'll maybe forgive me one day.*

Thinking about my own son and daughter and the multiple birthdays I've enjoyed with them, a deep ache in my heart pulsed at the notion of the pain Gypsy had to have felt over all she missed. I rested a hand on my heart as a few tears fell.

As I write this, I know I'll be going to live with Jesus soon. I really tore up my liver and my kidneys, and they did all they could do to fix me. Ain't nothing left now except to help the pain without making me a zombie again. But don't be sad for me. I'm excited to get to be in heaven, to see my own mama and daddy again, to see the babies I got rid of, and to have a clear head with no other voices. And I'll get to dance with Jesus on streets of gold! I don't know if you read the Bible much, but it says that when we get to heaven, there won't be no more crying, and God will wipe away all our tears. I think it's true, and I hope you believe it, too, because I want to see you and Danielle in Heaven (but only after your long life!)

I done sent Danielle her own letter. Maybe you can meet up and be brother and sister again. I think it would be special for both of you.

I had some dreams a couple months ago. I woke up in the middle of the night freaking out crying. In the dream was a little girl with short brown hair. She was underwater, crying for her mommy and daddy, but no one could hear her. Then things changed and that little girl was dead in a casket, and you were standing next to her crying. I woke up with my heart hurting so bad! Viola had been teaching me about how God can use dreams to get us to pray. Had no clue what I was praying for, but I knew somehow you were part of it. So I just prayed and prayed for days that whatever the devil had planned would be stopped. All those days I prayed, my heart was still hurting so bad. Then after about a week praying, I had another dream. That same little girl was holding hands with Jesus, and they were both smiling. When I had that second dream, I felt like God was telling me my prayers were answered, and all the hurt in my heart disappeared. I hope this doesn't sound crazy, but even if it does, I think it's important.

A soft sob erupted as I realized my own mother's role in interceding for Abigail's life. This thought was so massive, I wasn't even sure where to put it.

I'm not sure if you ended up with the kind of mama in your life who said good things to you, but I want to give you a blessing, as my son, from your mama. In Bible times, I guess it was a big deal for parents to speak good things to their kids on purpose. Even if I'd wanted to, I wouldn't have known how. But these are just Bible verses that I hope mean something to you. Viola helped me with this part.

May the Lord bless and keep you, may His face shine on you, may God turn His face to you and give you peace. May God give you whatever is in your heart, and help your plans go well. May Jesus make His home in your heart.

I do love you so much. XOXO – Gypsy.

Now my finger traces the lined pages of her letter as overwhelming love washes over me. Unable to contain that love, I clutch the priceless letter against my chest and allow myself to weep.

I was, and I am, a son who is loved.

26

AGE FORTY-NINE

G race's voice cracks as angry tears threaten. "But everything that happens on earth has been filtered through God's sovereign hand. He allows everything for a reason." Her shoulders slump, her palms up in a half-shrug. "I've heard it all my life. 'God is sovereign. God is in control. He works all things together for good. Everything that happens to me is filtered through God's permissive hand.'"

We sit on the sofa across from Marti again. Given the unexpected progress I seem to be making with Marti, we decided to cancel our monthly therapy appointments with Neil for now. Somehow her sessions leave me with a hope that I've never sensed with Neil.

I'm not sure I understand Marti's drive to help us, but I'm grateful. At least now I don't feel like punching someone as we sit here. Kendra is here with her clipboard as usual. I don't see Garrison, but I'm sure he's close by somewhere.

Marti is unruffled at Grace's challenge to her statement

that what has happened to me, to us, was not God's will. As I think about it, I must agree with Grace.

I lean forward in my most challenging, analytical pose. "Okay, so you're saying my childhood, all the abuse and the trauma, as well as what I'm going through with all of my blackouts and seeing and hearing things, you're saying these weren't part of God's plan for me?"

Marti smiles gently. "That's exactly what I'm saying, Danny."

Ready to take on this battle head-to-head, I sit up straight to launch my argument. "The entire book of Job proves you wrong. Job was perfect and sinless, and God dared satan to test him. So God orchestrated everything, and Job lost everything. So it must have been God's will."

Laying down her pen, Marti entwines her fingers. "Have you ever studied the scriptures through the original Hebrew or Greek?"

"I mean..." I falter. "Maybe a word here and there. But, if you mean like the whole Bible, no, I haven't done that." Kendra starts writing again and I choose to stop looking in her direction.

Marti continues. "You know, it's interesting how we read the Bible in America today. It actually wasn't written to us. The Bible we have today was written to the first century Jew. So we try to interpret scripture through our culture, a culture that values intellect and tells you to pull yourself up by your own bootstraps if you're down. When we do that, we get some of it wrong."

Glancing at Grace, I see her brow furrowed. Mine is too.

"I believe," Marti says, "through studies I have done and from teachers I have heard, that there's a ton of incorrect teaching about Job. And those teachings end up creating an image of God the Father as sadistic and cruel."

A scoff escapes me as a twinge of pain stabs my gut. "Isn't He?" I challenge. "Cruel, I mean. He seems hard-hearted to me sometimes."

Letting my statement pass, Marti leans forward. "I'm going to give you the high level of what I believe a deep study of the Hebrew actually says about Job. First of all, God didn't suggest that satan start to think about Job. God was calling satan out for how he was already planning to hurt Job. Second, Job himself walked in both fear and pride. He said that his greatest fear had come upon him. Fear is never of God, and it's an invitation for the enemy to bring what is feared. The text says that Job was also righteous in his own eyes. Sounds like pride to me. His children partied so hard that Job constantly offered sacrifices on their behalf. He fell into bitterness and self-pity, even cursing the day of his birth. Does that sound like a perfectly righteous and godly person to you? Third, the three men who called themselves Job's friends went on for days saying God had done all of this to Job because of some secret sin, but God rebuked Job's friends for saying those things. Had they been speaking truth, God wouldn't have rebuked them. And fourth, Job made a bunch of statements that are in total opposition to what Jesus said when He walked the earth. We often don't consider that even though the book of Job is written in the Bible, Job himself was actually wrong in what he said. God rebukes Job directly, Job repents, and then he's completely restored."

Heavy silence hangs in the room.

God, could this possibly be true?

My defense arsenal is nowhere near exhaustion. "Okay

then. What about Paul's thorn in the flesh? That physical malady or whatever it was that he struggled with. God never took that away from Paul, even when Paul begged Him to." Crossing my arms, I sit back smugly.

"Do you want an answer based on a dig into the original Greek which would negate your argument?" Marti offers with a kind smile. "Or are you looking for me to agree with you so that you can hold onto your beliefs?"

Somehow I don't feel threatened. It sounds more like an invitation. "I'd love to hear your perspective," I answer, surprised at my own discomfort.

"There are a few things about that passage we need to understand." Marti takes a quick gulp of her coffee and continues. "When Paul wrote about that thorn in the flesh, he said a messenger of satan was sent to buffet him. The word 'thorn' all through the Bible often referred to people, both in the Old Testament and in the New Testament. The word 'messenger' in the Greek, in every other use in scripture, referred to angels, demons, and people. The word 'buffet' in the Greek referred to torment and harassment. This thorn in the flesh was actually a person or a group of people in Paul's life who relentlessly persecuted him for his faith. Paul wasn't saying that he had a physical affliction. That's another teaching that I believe is false. And, just because the Lord didn't take it away from Paul does not mean it was from Him to begin with."

"Huh," Grace comments. Her brow still furrowed, she sits back and crosses her arms.

"And," Marti adds, "Paul wrote that this was done to keep him from being conceited. Maybe Paul knew how much he had walked in pride before his conversion. He makes an assumption that he would have been conceited, so possibly he concluded that this thorn in the flesh was to keep him humble. But think about it. Satan doesn't desire to make us humble, because true humility is a Christlike trait. And Paul may have been pretty awesome, but he wasn't infallible. I think he assumed that God wouldn't take the thorn away because he needed to remain humble. But the Lord Himself responded to Paul that His grace was sufficient. This is why Paul then wrote in the next verse that, '...for Christ's sake, I delight in weaknesses, in insults, in hardships, in persecutions, in difficulties. For when I am weak, then I am strong.' God was using the enemy's persecution of Paul to teach Paul total reliance and dependence upon Him. God did not persecute Paul, but God used that persecution to stretch Paul's faith."

Grace and I both stare at the ceiling as we try to wrap our minds around what we're hearing. Grace finally speaks softly. "What the enemy meant for evil, God has used for good."

"Exactly!" Marti points a finger at the air.

"Okay, what about this?" I point my finger in the air as well. "God closed Hannah's womb." I smirk, certain I've bested her this time.

Marti responds before I could sit back. "Hannah's womb was closed because God's law specifically promised barrenness in the land when the nation of Israel turned their back on God and walked in rebellion. The moment Hannah went to the temple in submission to the Lord, He opened her womb and she had Samuel within a year."

Grace and I both respond together. "Huh."

Silence hangs for another moment as we stare at the ceiling again. I risk a glance at Kendra. She stares at the ceiling, too.

"Let me ask you this question," asks Marti as she tucks

her legs underneath her. "Do you agree that the words of Jesus were always correct? If we think that something we've heard seems like it contradicts what Jesus Himself did or said, do you agree that Jesus would trump the contradiction?"

My brows lift as a quizzical frown forms. "What do you mean?"

Marti leans forward. "You know how people say, when a little girl dies of cancer for example, that God needed another angel in heaven, right? They say He must have had a plan to use the horrific pain of her parents for some greater good. We hear that all the time, even in church, right?"

I nod.

"If that's true," Marti taps the tips of her fingers together, "then why did Jesus raise anyone from the dead? Why is there not a single verse in the Bible where Jesus says something like, 'It was My Father's time for this one to die because others will see the deep faith of the traumatized family as they grieve well. So, I shall let this one stay dead.' Jesus never said or did anything like that. He raised every dead person who was brought to Him. So, if it was His Father's will that the person die, then Jesus would have been in opposition to His own Father's will by raising them from the dead."

Marti pauses for only a moment. "Jesus said verbatim, 'Satan came to steal, kill, and destroy, but I came to give abundant life.' He also said, 'If you've seen Me, you've seen the Father.' So from where I'm sitting, if anything even remotely looks like stealing, killing, or destroying, it absolutely is not God."

I open my mouth to form a retort, but nothing comes. Offense begins to rise in my belly. The words flow with difficulty. "I feel like everything I've been taught is a lie."

Glancing at her watch, Marti stretches out and stands. "I'm asking the two of you to accept a challenge. For the next thirty days, I want you to read just the four gospels and the book of Acts over and over again, as many times as you can in a month. I challenge you to find a single verse in those books that point to God bringing about anything that directly caused pain or death or destruction, or where Jesus refused to heal someone who was brought to Him. And the next time we get together, I want to hear what you discover."

Grace and I stand silently and gather our things as Marti places her hand on the doorknob. "Don't take my word for it," she says. "Search the scriptures for yourselves."

I take Grace's hand as we walk toward the parking lot. The bright August sun blinds me momentarily as we exit the building. As the sunlight hits me, I'm surprised to sense something else rising deep within my gut. It's unfamiliar and unexpected.

For the first time, perhaps ever in my life, I sense the budding presence of faith.

27

AGE FORTY-NINE

G asping for breath, I bolt upright and brush the flames from my arms.

Only there's no actual fire, and I'm in the dark in my own bed. I let out a long breath of relief.

It was just a dream.

Running my hands slowly down each of my forearms, I force my eyes to adjust to the lack of light.

If it was a dream, why does my left arm feel sunburned and sore?

After taking another long, slow breath, I run my hands through my hair and glance at the clock. It reads 1:11 a.m. Swinging my legs down to the floor, heart still racing, I slip out of bed to grab my bathrobe from the bedpost and tiptoe downstairs.

I've got to write this dream down. But first, coffee.

The aroma of the dark French roast pouring from the single-cup brewer makes my mouth water. Letting the delicious scent continue to calm me, I breathe deeply over the fresh mug and take that first delightful sip. "Thank You, God, for coffee. And I truly mean that."

Closing my office door softly, I tug the pull chain to turn on the floor lamp next to my desk. My office chair squeaks louder than I expect, so I try not to move much as I rifle through the top drawer for a pen and notepad.

Coffee, pen, and paper ready, and heart rate almost back to normal, I jot down each scene as it comes to mind.

The dream began with me in my counseling office at Kingston. Alone to start, I was working on several student files making notes and comparing computer data. Busy reading, writing, and typing, I sighed at the volume of work left to be done.

Then, Superintendent Ragsdale, Principal Miller, and Tanner Pike marched together into my office. All of them sneered as they chanted angrily in unison. "Look at you! Crazy loser! Crazy has a name, and it's Danny Pierce! Look at you! Crazy loser! Crazy has a name, and it's Danny Pierce!" Surrounding me on all sides, they pressed as their taunts grew deafening. The closer they got, the more their faces contorted until they each had fanged teeth.

Covering my ears, I jumped up and elbowed my way through them out the door. The chanting faded as Garrison, Kendra, Brody, and Tiny Tot met me in the hallway. Momentary relief flooded me at their familiarity. Coming alongside me, two on each side, they all linked arms and began to quickly lead me toward the auditorium doors.

"Why would you leave us?" asked Kendra. "Don't you love us? After all we've done for you and all we've been through together?"

I glanced at her sideways with my brows furrowed as we hustled down the hall. "What are you talking about?!"

Brody interrupted. "Yeah, man, not cool. We fought for you! We protected you! We've been there every time you needed us! Why would you just throw that away?"

I shook my head, almost tripping over my own feet as they propelled me faster toward the large double doors at the end of the hall. "I don't know what you mean!"

Tiny Tot started wailing. "Don't you love me, Danny? You can't leave me! EVERYONE LEAVES! You're not supposed to leave!"

Panic began to rise up. "I don't understand!" I shouted as bewilderment threatened to drop me to my knees.

"We know what you're doing, Danny," said Garrison, "and we can't allow it. We need to protect you from yourself."

Instead of continuing to walk alongside me in a line of camaraderie, Brody and Garrison began to roughly drag me forward. Stumbling from the force, I struggled and twisted against them, but they continued to pull me back toward the auditorium.

At the sight of the double doors, I planted my feet hard.

In the cracks all around the doorframe, flames of fire shot into the hall. And standing at the door with a palm on the handle, his red-headed face in a demonic grin, stood a teenage version of Carl Blackwell. He let out a maniacal laugh as he moved to open the door.

Blocking my eyes with my hands, I screamed at the top of my lungs. "JESUS! HELP ME!"

Before I could finish getting my words out, a sonic boom reverberated through the space. The percussive depth of the explosion sent a cool blast through my being. Turning around, everyone's jaw dropped at the sight of the large doorway at the opposite end of the hall.

Blinding, spectacular beams of bluish-white light emanated from the center of the doorway. Squinting and shielding my eyes, I struggled to make sense of what I saw. An eight-foot-tall outline of a being stood silhouetted against the radiant light, and this being had a massive set of wings protruding from its shoulders.

This was an angel.

Shaking myself from the grip of Brody and Garrison, I took off running toward the angel with everything I had. Crying desperate sobs of "Help me!" over and over, I ran and ran. But the angel wasn't getting any closer. My feet were running, but I wasn't moving forward.

Glancing over my shoulder, I screamed at Garrison and Brody who each still held a corner of my shirt. "Let me go!"

The fiery auditorium door was propped fully open as Carl stood in front of the inferno sneering at me and laughing. Flames began to leap past Carl and connect with the Others. But the fire didn't consume them. It just danced along their arms and legs with a life of its own.

I turned back to the angel, sobbing and hysterical. "PLEASE! HELP ME!" I continued to try to wrestle myself from my captors, but went nowhere as the heat behind me became unbearable. The acrid scent of burning sulfur assaulted my nose and stung my eyes.

In a flash, the angel closed the distance between us. I couldn't look directly at it for the blinding light radiating from its head. Massive arms wrapped in ornate metallic sleeves reached out and grabbed one of my wrists and began to tug. The air around the angel swirled with mesmerizing bands of blue and silver, and the cool smell of cedar wafted through my senses.

Grabbing my other wrist from behind, Brody fastened a painful grip with both of his hands. "Not today, Danny-boy!" he taunted. "You belong to us!"

I watched in horror as the flame dancing along Brody's shoulders began to flow down his arms onto my skin. The smell of burning flesh stung my nose as I screamed in agony.

A raging war cry erupted from the depths of my belly as I turned back to the angel. "JESUS! I! WANT! MY! FREEDOM!"

At my final word, I launched myself with every fiber of my being toward that angel. I instantly felt an armored pair of well-muscled arms wrap around me and draw me toward safety. As I dared to look into the angel's crystal blue eyes, he spoke to me without moving his lips. "It won't be long now, Danny." Then I buried my head into his chest and everything began to fade.

The last thing I remember hearing was Tiny Tot screaming my name. "DANNY, DON'T GO!"

Now, I sit back and drain the last few drops of my coffee as I read my dream over again.

Grace isn't gonna believe this. If I even tell her. I would sound so stupid.

I'm not even sure I believe it.

What could this mean?

28

AGE FORTY-NINE

"I t's no big deal, dude," says the Bossman. "You're fine. Chill out."

I pace up and down the sidewalk in front of my favorite coffee shop. Bluegrass Café knows how to make the perfect cup, and the neon-colored patio seating and instrumental jazz music make for a fun, funky environment. A comfortably cool, early September breeze rustles the nearby shrubs with the promise of autumn wafting through the air.

The music does little to settle me. I pause to check myself again in the reflection of the coffee shop window as the wind whips my hair.

Why am I so nervous to meet my very own sister? And why did I tell her I'd wear this bulky University of Kentucky Wild-cats jersey? I look like a frat boy wannabe.

Several weeks after receiving Gypsy's letter, another letter had come in the mail. I'd been puttering around the house all day, replacing light bulbs, caulking bathrooms, tightening fixtures, and doing all kinds of other tasks I'd put off for months.

As I stood back to admire the handiwork of my freshly-fixed mailbox flag, the postal truck rolled up with a stack of mail held out the window.

"Thanks, Theo!" I said as I accepted the small mail bundle. Flipping through the envelopes, I sorted as I headed straight to the recycling bin.

"Junk. Ads. Don't need a home equity loan. Oh good, there's the new insurance cards I've been waiting for. Junk. More junk."

A small pink envelope with handwritten lettering almost slipped out of my hands. Tossing the useless mail into the recycling bin, I looked more closely at the return address written in beautiful cursive script.

Danielle Zeigler
2911 Joshua Trace,
Cincinnati, OH 03160

That's odd. The only Danielle I know is...
It can't be.

Heart in my throat, I headed into the house and went straight to my office. Laying the envelope on the desk, I ran my fingers over the writing. A smile crept into the corners of my mouth as images of my sister flooded my mind.

Taking a deep breath, I sliced into the top of the envelope with my letter knife and pulled out the single folded piece of pink stationery.

Dear Danny,

I hope it's okay that I'm writing. I got your address from Mom's last letter to me. She mentioned you'd received a letter as well and that maybe we might consider getting together. I know it's kind of out of the blue after all this time, but I prayed about it and felt like God wanted me to reach out.

I'd love to meet up for coffee or something, but only if you want to. I'm living in Cincinnati now, so it's not that far of a drive.

Whenever you feel like it, you can reach me at the email or cell number at the bottom. I got your number from Mom's nursing home, so it's stored in my phone in case you call or text me. And there's truly no pressure if it's not the right time.

I do want you to know that I'm praying for you.

Love, your sister Danielle

It took me several weeks to muster up the courage to reply with an email, and several more weeks to agree on a date. And now I'm here at our designated meeting spot, unsure why I'm so terrified.

As I continue to stare at myself in the coffee shop glass, I sense movement to my right. The window reflects a woman with long, dark hair in an Ohio State jersey standing next to me.

A soft voice greets me. "Hi Danny."

Suddenly five years old inside, I fight back several sobs as I turn toward my sister and lean into her. As kids I was always the shorter one, so my half a foot of higher stature makes for an awkward embrace. But I don't care, and neither does she.

We stand like this for several minutes without a word, both of us weeping softly. A crick forming in my neck forces me to break away. I take a deep breath and clear my throat.

"Wanna sit?" I ask.

Slipping into the fluorescent green bistro seats, we face each other and hold hands across the table. Kendra steps behind Danielle, clipboard and pen ready.

My sister and I both start to speak at the same time, and we both chuckle.

"Wow," Danielle starts. "I just can't believe that we're actually here together. It's surreal."

I nod. "Ha, yeah, that's a good word for it. Definitely surreal."

A teenage server with purple hair and a nose ring breezes up to our table. "What can I get y'all?"

I motion my hand for Danielle to order first.

She taps the menu. "I'd love a chai latte with almond milk and a cranberry scone, please."

"And I'll have the bulletproof Americano and a cinnamon roll."

Danielle laughs as the server heads to the next table. "Still the sweet tooth, huh?"

A sheepish grin crosses my face as I shrug.

She folds her hands on the table. "So. Is there anything you'd like to know? Ask me anything at all."

Propping my elbows on the table and resting my chin on my clasped fingers, I clear my throat. "Okay, then. Let's see. So, your last name is Zeigler. I saw that on the letter. Is that a married name?"

She smiles. "Yeah, it is. Married my high school sweetheart. His name is Brad. We went to Ohio State together, and we got married the day after graduation. We have five kids..."

"FIVE kids!? Holy smokes, that's a lot of laundry!"

"Haha, yeah, he was from a large family, and all of his siblings had a ton of kids. I've loved every minute of it. Brad has always loved the Lord, and he's been the most amazing husband and dad. Our youngest is twelve, and we actually just married off our oldest this summer."

Sweet gratitude fills my eyes. "That's so awesome. I'm so happy for you. That's wild that you're somebody's mother-in-law now."

She nods and snickers. "I know, right? I don't feel that old. So, what about you?"

"Well, I definitely got a later start. But I'm married to my wife Grace. We actually met at church when I was twenty-seven. She's an angel and a saint and I don't deserve her. We have two kids; Josiah just turned nine, and Abigail is almost five. They're awesome little people. In a lot of ways, they've been a godsend like they'll never understand. I love them so much my heart aches sometimes, but I also haven't been the most stable dad. I'm working on it, though."

Pastries and coffees appear in front of us as the server delivers our order and scoots off again.

"Wow, that was fast," I say as I start to lift the gooey roll to my lips. Danielle closes her eyes and bows her head, so I return the pastry to the plate and lick my fingers.

"Lord Jesus," she starts. "Thank You doesn't seem like enough. But thank You for bringing us together today. Jesus, come be with us. And we ask You to bless this food. In Your holy name, amen."

"Amen," I agree as I dive into the warm, melty sweet goodness. Following my first bite with a long swig of delicious coffee, I close my eyes to savor the treat.

Danielle enjoys a few of her own bites then clears her throat. "So were you in any kind of contact with Mom before she passed?"

I grab a napkin and wipe frosting from my lips. "Nah. Last time I saw her, I think it was at least fifteen years ago. She was pretty out of it. She didn't recognize me. She wasn't all there, you know? It was heartbreaking. What about you?"

She looks skyward as she thinks for a moment. "I guess the last time I saw her face to face was maybe three years ago. She was a completely different person from the times I'd seen her before, so much so that I almost didn't recognize her. It sounds crazy but she had this peaceful glow about her. She told me all about Viola leading her to the Lord and discipling her. She was present and coherent, and she could actually remember things. She even put her hand on my head and blessed me."

I smile. "Yeah, she wrote me a blessing in the letter she sent me."

After finishing our breakfast in comfortable silence, we both swap our depleted drinks for water. Danielle leans forward with clasped hands.

"So tell me. How are you? Like really, how are you doing?"

"Careful, Danny," warns the Bossman. "She's basically a stranger. Keep your guard up."

Sitting back, I rub my chin and run my hand through my hair. Sweat begins to pour, so I pull off the heavy Wildcats jersey for the comfort of my T-shirt underneath. A soft breeze blows past.

"You know, I'm surprised to hear myself say this, but I'm doing better now than I have been for probably most of my life. I'll spare you the details, but it turns out that Gypsy, I mean Mom, she and I had a few things in common on the mental side."

Kendra scowls in my direction.

Her brows furrowed, Danielle places a hand on top of mine. "Oh, Danny, I'm so sorry to hear that. I didn't know."

I shrug. "Yeah, it became critical there for a while. But Grace and I are in this new church that's nothing like any church I've been to before. They've just opened wide their hearts to love us well. And you mentioned discipleship, they're like the apostles in Acts. And I've started meeting with this woman who does something called inner healing prayer. She's helped me more than years of therapy and counseling. I mean, I still say I'm crazy, and I have a long way to go. But I can feel things starting to shift a little bit."

Squeezing my hand, she smiles. "That's fantastic! I'm so glad you shared that with me. Now I understand why the Lord has been prompting me to pray for you for so long."

I flush at the thought of the Lord bringing *me* to someone else's mind for prayer.

Danielle releases my hand. Reaching into her purse, she

pulls out a thick business envelope and slides it across the table with a sweet smile.

"So one of the reasons I wanted to meet with you is to make sure you received this. Turns out Mom had a life insurance policy."

My jaw drops as I place my hand on the package. "I... I... what?"

"Yeah, I was shocked, too. A lawyer reached out to me like a week after she died. The way she had it set up, it was an immediate payout split between the two of us."

Heart instantly pounding, I fumble to release the flap. I eventually resort to just tearing the top seam away, and I slide the contents in front of me.

The top document is a short letter from a lawyer's office addressed to me expressing condolences and referencing an enclosed check.

A sob escapes me as I set the letter aside and glance at the check made payable to me.

Twenty thousand dollars!

I cover my eyes with the check, unable to stem the tears.

Tiny Tot's voice brings me into focus. "Danny, are you okay? What's happening?"

Wiping my tears with one hand and motioning Tiny Tot away with the other, I take a long, deep breath.

"Wow, sorry about that."

Danielle smiles softly. "You have nothing to apologize for. I did the same thing."

I release a grateful laugh. "It's just, I actually lost my job earlier this year. So, as you can imagine, finances have been kind of a mess. The timing of this couldn't be more perfect."

Picking up the check again, I read the numbers several times over to be sure the first one wasn't a mirage. I start to giggle as I calculate the balances on some of the larger bills we've been dodging.

Danielle clasps her hands on the table. "Danny, I'm sure that Mom was pretty transparent in her last letter to you. I know she was very honest and open in my letter. But I want you to know that the last time I spoke on the phone with her, she talked about you with such love. I think we've both figured out that she was pretty messed up when we came along, but when we got taken away, she shattered. I think I understand a little more now how much she carried that woundedness through her life."

Pain shoots through my heart. All I can do is nod my head.

"She reminded me of a comical story about us if you want to hear it."

I grin. "Sure, I'd love to."

She's already laughing. "So I guess you had just turned two, so I would have been seven. Sometimes Mom would let me walk you to this trashy park a couple of block away. This one time you decided to wander over to the little patch of shrubs along the back fence line. I lost you for a second, and then I heard you saying 'kitty!' You crawled out holding this little ball of black and white fuzz, and you just kept saying 'kitty' over and over. Well, I just assumed you'd found a kitten."

"Uh-oh," I laugh. "I bet I can guess where this is going!"

"I knew there was no way Mom would be okay with keeping a kitten. So I told you we had to keep it a secret. We snuck in with it stuffed down in my shirt, and we made it a little bed in the back of the closet. It looked kinda weird, so I decided it must have had a birth defect."

I smile at the images forming in my mind.

"We kept that deformed kitty alive for over a week before Mom figured out why we'd suddenly started taking snacks to our room. You and I were on the floor in the closet feeding this thing some macaroni, and Mom ripped the door open. But that scared the kitty, which, turns out, wasn't actually a kitty. It was a skunk, and it sprayed both of us!"

I clap my hands and roar with laughter. "Oh no!"

"She had to soak us in tomato juice four times to get that smell off! She had to throw out every single piece of clothing in that closet. I mean, as a parent, can you imagine? We didn't get into trouble, though."

"I wonder if that's why I'm not a fan of cats?"

She laughs again. "That's entirely possible."

Glancing at her watch, Danielle finishes off her water. "Well, I hate to leave but I've got to be at the school for a parent-teacher conference." Pausing, she considers me for a moment. "Would it be okay if I pray for you before I go?"

Frowning, Kendra crosses her arms behind Danielle. I ignore her.

"Sure, that'd be great," I say as I sit forward and bow my head.

The touch of my sister's hand on my shoulder surprises me.

She takes a deep breath. "Lord, I thank You. Thank You for bringing me and Danny together after all this time. Thank You for the beautiful gift of salvation, and we are so grateful

CRAZY HAS A NAME

that You sent Viola to Mom. We know beyond a shadow of a doubt that Mom is fully whole and healed with You, and that because we know You, we'll get to see Mom again."

Grateful tears pool at the thought of Gypsy enjoying heaven with perfect mental clarity.

"Lord, I lift up my brother Danny to You. Thank You for the journey You've had him on, and I bless that journey. Thank You for leading him to his new church, and for orchestrating the people in his life who are coming alongside him."

Lifting her hand from my shoulder, Danielle places both of her palms on the top of my head. With her touch comes a beautiful sense of calm.

"Lord, I speak a special blessing over Danny's brain, his mind, and his thoughts. I cover every synapse, every neural pathway, and every neurotransmitter with the powerful blood of Jesus Christ. I call them into perfect function on earth as it is in heaven. I bless his brain with alignment and unity of mind, and I bless every molecule with peace. And Lord, I ask You to continue to show Danny just how much You love him. In Jesus' name, amen."

A brief sensation of something like warm oil emanates from the top of my head and down to my neck as a beautiful quietness washes over me.

Wow.

Reaching down from behind to wrap her arms around me, Danielle gives me a big squeeze.

"I gotta run," she says. "Let's plan for a longer visit soon, okay? It'd be amazing if our families could hang out."

I stand and return the hug. "Absolutely. That'd be awesome. I'll check with Grace."

Cupping my face in her hands, she smiles at me with pure love. "I'm incredibly proud of you, Danny. And I'm gonna keep on praying for you until you tell me to stop. And even then, I'll probably keep praying."

Please never stop.

29

AGE FORTY-NINE

"Three or four *hours*? How can one person possibly need a prayer for that long?"

My brow furrowed, I glance up at Grace as I pour myself a sweet tea refill. Grace's parents have the kids for bowling and pizza, so Grace and I enjoy a rare quiet meal together in our dining room. She's made my favorite—eggplant parmigiano with a creamy Caesar salad and cheesy garlic bread. She tells me she's made some kind of discipleship counseling prayer appointment, whatever that means, with a minister recommended by Marti.

"I know, that's what I said," she answers before taking a bite of salad. "Here's how Leah from my women's Bible study group explained it."

Kendra is in the background. She gazes around the room in disinterest as Grace begins to explain.

"They don't just sit and pray with you. I mean, yes, that's a big part of it. But Leah called it a thorough format healing prayer."

My fork cuts perfectly into the bready, saucy eggplant. "Sounds a little woo-woo to me," I say.

"I thought so, too," she answers. "But it sounds like a mix of counseling and praying. I guess the first hour or two is spent on answering a ton of questions about my history. Like, any problems with my birth, what my early home life was like, did I have any mean teachers or creepy uncles, background like that."

Kendra positions her clipboard to write. I ignore her as I swallow a bite and let Grace continue.

"Then we talk about any stupid stuff I may have done, like playing with Ouija boards or dabbling in voodoo as a kid. Plus I guess we'll talk about boyfriends from my past, any friends who became enemies, and people who I feel betrayed me."

The Bossman whispers, "Past boyfriends? What do we think about that, Danny-boy?"

I take a quick sip of tea. "Boyfriends, huh?" I ask. I sound more offended than I feel.

Grace pats the top of my hand. She doesn't take the bait. "I've already told you about every single guy I ever dated, Danny. Even if we only had one date. I have no secrets from you. The reason we talk about it is to make sure I'm not holding onto any old bitterness or pain, or to see if I started believing any lies about myself because of how I was treated."

"Huh," I say. "Guess I never thought about it like that."

"I know, right?" she says. I cannot deny her eagerness as she continues. "There's also lots of questions they'll ask me around trauma, like traumas I went through as a kid, or any big incidents in adulthood."

Out of the corner of my eye, I catch Garrison walk up next

to Kendra as a small stab stings my gut. "Like, including what I've caused from being crazy?" I ask quietly.

Laying down her fork, Grace shifts toward me and lays her hand on top of mine. "You know I don't call you that word, sweetie," she says softly. "Will I probably talk about some of the big things you and I have gone through while I'm there? Sure. But that's not why I'm going to this appointment."

"So why then are you going exactly?"

A beautiful combination of peace and wonder comes over Grace's countenance as she answers. "It's the testimonies I've heard from Leah and Debbie and some of the other ladies in the study group who have all done this same kind of healing prayer at this same place. Like, they talk about how they never knew some of the emotional baggage they'd been carrying until they went through it all, and God showed them the lies they were believing. Debbie said she'd never been able to talk about how her six-year-old granddaughter died four years ago without collapsing into a sobbing heap on the ground. But somehow through this kind of prayer, she was finally able to let go of all the pain and the grief and the need to know why. Like something major shifted in her. Ever since I've known her, there was always this cloud of sadness over her. But it's not there anymore. We all noticed it when she walked into Bible study last month."

She stops to enjoy a big bite of garlic bread, and I continue to savor my dinner as I try to let her words sink in. I'm not sure where to put them.

"And there's this other lady," she continues. "Her name is Eliza. I don't think you've met her. She's a super sweet lady, probably at least ten years younger than me, but we could always tell how much she hated herself. She's quite over-weight, and she doesn't take care of herself. She would always make comments about how dumb she was, and put herself down. And she said last year she was diagnosed with Crohn's disease. When she went in for her healing prayer, for the first time in her life she told them about the things her older brother used to do to her when she was little. I guess her mom definitely knew about it, but her mom said that boys will be boys and that Eliza needed to make it stop. At eight years old she was told this!"

Garrison clears his throat and takes a few steps closer to me. Breathing long and slow, I shift toward Grace and away from Garrison.

I don't need you right now.

"So anyway," Grace says, "Eliza was finally able to forgive her brother for what he did, and her mom for letting it go on, and then she forgave herself because she'd blamed herself all these years. She said it was such a profound experi-ence that she's even noticing her Crohn's symptoms are starting to go away. She's stopped making all of the negative comments about herself, and she just seems so content now."

Interesting.

"I know it's a long afternoon by yourself with the kids," she adds.

I hadn't considered that. Grace hasn't trusted me alone with the kids for several years now.

"It'll be fine," I lie. "It's just one afternoon."

She smiles as she stands to start clearing the dinner table. "I've already asked my mom if she can bring pizza for all of you while I'm there. She can stay here and play games with them."

So I'm too crazy to even just be a dad alone with my own kids.

Deep shame rises as my failure with Abigail and Josiah last week comes to mind. Lost in my turmoil, I had completely forgotten that they were outside playing while Grace ran a quick errand, and I locked the doors and laid down for a nap. Josiah smartly decided to walk down the block with a terrified Abigail to his friend's house. Their parents called Grace who immediately rescued the kids and burst through our door for a well-deserved lecture.

What kind of person forgets about their own kids?

Kendra takes a few notes.

"I'm sure they'll love that," I answer as guilt creeps over me. "That'll give me time to finally rake leaves if it doesn't rain."

"So it does." She kisses me on the top of my head as she carries our plates to the kitchen sink.

It all sounds well and good. So why am I anxious?

The cool October wind raises a slight chill on my skin as I rake massive leaf piles around the backyard. I enjoy getting lost in the yard-taming process, mowing and raking and lopping off wayward branches. In many ways I find it therapeutic.

I may not be able to control much, but this, I can control.

The nervousness in my body causes me to be extra aggressive with the yard work today. I intentionally try not to ponder what Grace is doing or saying about me right now, but I repeatedly fail.

She's going for herself. It's not about me. Focus on the dead leaves. Missed a spot!

"It's all good, man," the Bossman whispers. "You're fine, just like you've always been fine."

I'm fine. Am I?

Blowing out hard, I want to start arguing with the Bossman about the definition of being "fine." But Grace's car pulling into the driveway redirects my attention. I finish up the last few passes of raking and hang the rake back in the tool shed.

Grace meets me just inside the back gate. Her eyes are red from crying, but her expression is far from sad.

She is utterly radiant.

This is unexpected.

I try to protest that I'm sweaty and dirty as she falls into me in a tender embrace. Clearly she doesn't care how I look or smell at the moment. Wrapping my arms around her, we hold each other for several long minutes. She finally draws back and pulls both of my hands into hers, entwining our fingers.

"You know what the Lord told me today?" she asks, new tears brimming. Her voice is a mix of whispered awe and secret childhood wonder. "He called me his beautiful beloved bride. Little old me. Gracie Evelyn Pierce. *His beloved bride!*"

Somewhere in the back of my memory, the concept of a Bible verse floats up.

"Oh yeah?" I ask. "So what else did He say?"

She inhales a long breath. "He said I've been released from all of the false responsibility I've been carrying around, always trying to fix everyone. Fixing you, fixing our kids, fixing my parents. He showed me how much I had taken all that on as a burden. But once He showed me where I first started doing that, which wasn't where I thought it was, I was able to forgive it and release that responsibility back to the people who didn't realize they were putting it on me. I actually heard this internal voice, like Jesus was talking directly to me. He said, 'Gracie, that's My job. You're free from believing you'll somehow be held accountable for other people's choices.'"

The joy on her face as she shares this revelation surprises me. I've known this about her for years, but she could never hear me when I brought it up.

Amazing.

My eyes divert to the dirt as shame and guilt creep across my cheeks. "I'm sure you talked about my craziness, huh? About how much garbage I've put you and the kids through?"

She takes my hand. "Yes, we did talk about you some, but not in the way you're asking. It wasn't to label or criticize you; it was more about learning how to release it all to Jesus."

"So, it was a good meeting then?" Her demeanor moves me, but I'm at a loss to offer much more.

She pulls me toward the house. "So good," she says. "Definitely different than what I expected, and I still have a lot to process. It wasn't anything like the counseling we've been going to with Neil. I mean I think we've had progress with him, don't get me wrong. But for one thing, it seems like we're just getting started on an issue and poof! Fifty-five minutes is up, see you next week. And, I know Neil is a Christian, but this lady I met with today, Theresa, she talks to the Lord like nobody I've ever heard before, even at church. She's more like Marti. She just talks to Him like you talk to a best friend. I feel like I've been taught what real prayer is supposed to be like, and it's... I don't know. More authentic? Transparent? It's hard to describe. But I definitely know this. I feel completely different inside."

Great. Someone else more spiritual than me.

"Well, I'm glad it was a good time," I say as we walk in through the back door.

Just don't ask me to do anything like that.

30

AGE FORTY-NINE

Why didn't I let him die? It's what he deserved!
        I can barely feel the ground beneath my feet as I
trudge along the cold, isolated sidewalk in the dark. Suburban
Halloween decorations of skeletons and graveyard markers
match the dark brooding in my spirit.

A fleeting thought races through my mind, almost too
quickly to catch, but unmistakable just the same.

"I haven't given you what you deserved, Danny."

I look around expecting to see Garrison or Kendra, but
I'm alone.

The evening had started out fairly normally. I had come
home exhausted from a job networking event and plopped
into my recliner to watch college football highlights. Grace
made sure dinner was ready early since Abigail had a skating
party and Josiah had soccer practice. Knowing how anxious I
get these days if I'm driving anywhere after dark, Grace
kissed me on the cheek before she headed out with the kids. I

tried not to let the disappointment in Josiah's face hurt my heart, but it stung.

Thirty minutes of flipping through mindless television channels wouldn't do a thing for the boredom. So I changed into some sweatpants and set off for the North Elkhorn River-walk Park.

My mind was bombarded with all of the events of the past year. Aimee's case. Carl's involvement. Being suspended. Gypsy. My own craziness.

I am such a loser!

No matter how fast my feet walked, my mind ran harder as the sun began to descend toward the horizon. Trotting down the curved stairs of Riverwalk Park that dipped under the overpass bridge, I veered off and headed toward the water in search of a mental diversion. I was so focused on the thought storm that I almost didn't hear the screeching tires and collision of metal as a red SUV burst through the guardrail of the overpass above me. Almost in slow motion, the nose of the car dove the thirty feet straight down from the bridge, smacking hard into the water just ahead of me.

Frozen in horror, I watched as the car bobbed up and down, then tipped forward and splashed down onto its roof, wheels up and still spinning in the air. A nearby jogger had heard the commotion and darted past me toward the water.

"Hey, man," he yelled. "We gotta try and help them!"

My arms and legs were paralyzed as I stared at the sinking car. Then the jogger's voice finally connected in my brain, and I followed him into the murky, frigid water. Already the upside-down SUV was almost halfway underwater and drop-ping. It only took a moment of running through the water for the river bottom to fall away beneath me, and we swam as hard as we could to reach the car. By the time we did, bubbles surrounded us, and the vehicle was over halfway submerged and disappearing fast.

The jogger kicked and pulled his way to the other side of the car. Then he shouted, "I'm gonna try to open the driver's side door! Can you see anyone in the back seat?"

Nodding with a deep breath, I dove under the chilly water. The car's impact had stirred up a swirl of sand and silt, so much so that I could barely make anything out. Doing my best to ignore the burning in my eyes, I groped until the SUV's outline was inches in front of me. Finally getting my bearings, I pressed my face to the glass of the back door. I could make out the gushing of water into the back seat, but thankfully it looked empty except for some papers and a large pair of shoes. Moving to look through the front passenger window, I saw only some trash swirling in the flood.

Lungs burning, I resurfaced and gulped in the fresh air. The other rescuer popped up and shouted, "Anything on that side?" I shook my head no.

"I need help to get this guy out!" he yelled. "I'm not strong enough!"

Swimming around to the front of the car, I realized how young and small the jogger was, and how much bigger I was in comparison. He wasn't much more than a kid.

The entire car was already beneath the surface. We didn't have much time.

"What's your name?" I shouted above the racket.

"Zack. The driver's window is broken and he's not wearing a seatbelt, so we should be able to just reach in and pull him out."

I nodded. "Ready?" I asked.

"Ready!" Shoulder to shoulder, we both took a massive breath and sank back down.

Still swirling with silt and debris, the cloudy water made everything seem far away. I felt along the outer wheel well until I could finally distinguish the outline of the door and then the open window. A man was slumped over the steering wheel, and his head was badly cut open.

Reaching through the broken window, my hand found the belt of his pants. I wedged my fingers under the belt, and drawing my knees up, I braced my feet against the car and pulled backward with all I had.

As I pulled the man up, the weight of the fully submerged SUV pulled the vehicle downward to the riverbed away from me. The jagged edge of the broken car window raked along the outside of my arm as the car slipped down. Gripping the unconscious man's belt while Zack grasped under his armpit, we both kicked hard for the surface.

The air was crisp and sweet as I gulped several big breaths. Coughing and sputtering, Zack and I finally found the riverbed firm under our feet.

"We got you man! We got you!" Zack kept shouting.

Linking our hands across the man's back, each of us draped one of his arms across our shoulder as we limped up out of the water and onto the sandy bank, dragging the victim between us. My leg muscles were screaming, and the slice along my arm burned hot.

Kendra stood off to my left. I ignored her.

Crawling on hands and knees, we eased the injured man face down onto the ground. I could tell he wasn't breathing.

Between coughs, I asked Zack, "Do you know CPR?" Breathing hard, he shook his head no.

Ripping off the bottom hem of my T-shirt, I wrapped it around the open gash on my arm. "We gotta get the water out of his lungs," I said as I pressed down on the man's back. "Here, help me roll him over."

Straddling his bloated belly, I positioned my hands atop each other at the base of the man's sternum and started compressions. I had pressed only a few times when I finally glanced up at the man's face, framed by thick, red hair.

It was Carl Blackwell.

Swallowing hard several times to keep from vomiting all over his face, I fought to stay present as the edges of my vision grew swirly. A thought passed through my mind. "Would you want to die this way?"

Zack's voice broke through the haze. "Hey man, what are you doing? Keep going!"

In my mind's eye, I grabbed Carl by the hair and shook him violently while screaming at the top of my lungs. "You filthy scum! How many lives have you destroyed, Carl?! How much did you get paid to make kiddie videos! You nasty, perverted freak! Death is too good for you! You deserve to burn in hell!"

Zack shook my shoulder. "What's wrong man?! He's gonna die if you don't help him!"

I heard the fleeting thought again. "Would you want to die this way? What would that do to Grace?"

As Grace came to mind, I felt an inexplicable power overtake me. I immediately jumped off of Carl and knelt beside his head. Lifting his chin with one hand and plugging his nose with the other, I blew several sharp breaths into his mouth. Then I straddled him again and restarted the CPR.

As I pressed hard on Carl's sternum, I glanced at his limp

arm and saw three small cigarette burn circles in the shape of a triangle. A fleeting whisper of pity raced by, but I refused to give it purchase.

"You deserve to die," I continued to whisper under my breath with every compression. "You deserve to die. You deserve to die."

As the sound of sirens reached my ears, suddenly Carl's abdomen heaved. Flipping him onto one side away from me, dirty river water gushed out of his mouth as he wretched and gagged. He was going to make it.

I had just saved the life of the man who helped destroy mine.

My gut threatened to heave again, so I stumbled to the tree line by the sidewalk while paramedics rushed to tend to Carl. Hot tears wanted to come, but the swelling rage wouldn't let them.

The setting sun cast a fiery orange glow across the horizon as I started walking. I didn't know where to go, but I had to go somewhere. I barely registered the shouts of Zack and a paramedic calling after me.

My soaking wet clothes clinging to my chilled skin, I walked aimlessly for hours. The waning daylight turned dusky, muting the landscape around me as streetlights began to flicker to life. Still I walked. Diehard cyclists and evening dog-walkers eventually gave way to deserted streets as I continued under a cloudless night sky.

Why didn't I let him die? It's what he deserved.

"I haven't given you what you deserved, Danny."

"Who said that?" I asked aloud. I fully expected the Bossman or Garrison to answer.

The thought repeated. It came from a different place than

the voices of the Others. "I haven't given you what you deserved, Danny."

At the sound of my own name, I knew.

"Oh God," I said, my heart pounding and painful anger continuing to boil. "I've never raped any little kids! I've never made videos of kids doing nasty things! That's what Carl did, in case You forgot!"

The sense of injustice threatened to blind me.

A gentle thought flowed into my mind. "Do you remember your life before you met Me, Danny?"

Now as I've walked until my feet ache, I have nothing to say.

Recognizing the entrance to my own darkened, quiet neighborhood, I drag myself down the sidewalk to my driveway. As I reach the front step and fumble with the lock, Grace flings the door open, her face flooded with anger and accusation at my return after hours without calling. Her scolding halts mid-sentence as my bloody arm and muddy clothes come into the light. Her rage turns to loving concern in an instant.

I melt into her embrace and weep.

31

AGE FORTY-NINE

"All Rise! All Rise! The honorable Judge Jackson presiding," the thick-waisted bailiff calls.

The shuffling and stretching of over one hundred people fills the ornately crafted old courtroom as we all stand. The movement stirs up the latent dust, and I watch a transparent, swirling cloud as it dances through the wide afternoon sunbeam streaming from a pair of high transom windows. Despite the rays of sun, the early November winds manage to sneak through the corners and cracks of the room, lending a welcome chill to the crowded air.

The judge breezes into his seat and mumbles, "You may be seated." His delivery diminishes the gravity and serious-ness of the verdict at hand. Participating in the rectification of decades of injustice impacting many hundreds of innocent victims, or ordering a tuna salad sandwich and a root beer – he could be doing either from my perspective.

I am grateful to even be permitted in the room. My attorney was kind enough to smooth things over for me with the court given my diagnosis. I still had to make her a million promises, but she understands why I need to be here.

Garrison, Kendra, Brody, and Tiny Tot stand in a huddle in the back corner of the courtroom. They all watch me closely, awaiting the verdict to come. Aimee catches my eye and we exchange little waves, her electric green bangs peeking out from under a black bandana. Now that I've been officially fired, I'm no longer prohibited from interacting with her. Jaw set, she nods at me. She's ready.

Judge Jackson looks down at his notes as he asks, "Ladies and gentlemen of the jury, have you selected a foreman?"

An older gentleman with overalls and a bowtie stands. "Yes, Your Honor, we have. My name is Winston Gartrell, Your Honor."

The judge removes his eyeglasses and scans the crowd. "Now I wish to remind everyone present here today that this is a joinder case. This means that, while all of the proceedings up until now have been evaluated as a whole, there are separate individual defendants in this case. Each one of these defendants will receive their own separate verdict and their own individual sentencing if they are found guilty."

Judge Jackson pauses as he continues to scan the room. Spotting me, he bores a hole between my eyes as he continues. "I will ask all of you in attendance here today to please control yourselves as the verdicts are delivered. I will not tolerate theatrics and outbursts in my courtroom, and my bailiffs are ready to respond with force. Anyone disrupting these proceedings will be escorted from the room immediately and charged with contempt of court with the maximum allowable penalty. I trust that I make myself clear."

I nod and swallow hard.

Replacing his eyeglasses, he looks at the defense attorney. "Would all of the defendants please rise?"

Vincent Petrenko, Brenda Jo Starnes, and Carl Blackwell all stand. Carl's suit is two sizes too small and he is in desperate need of a shave. He stares at the floor, hands clasped at his protruding belly.

Unexpected pity seeps into my heart, but it's followed quickly by anger.

Judge Jackson asks, "Mr. Foreman, has the jury reached a unanimous decision in each of the counts presented?" He still looks down at his papers, quite interested in whatever he's reading.

"Yes we have, Your Honor."

"Bailiff, would you please retrieve the verdict from the Foreman?"

The room falls silent as Judge Jackson opens the verdict form and clears his throat.

"In the first count of cruelty to children, we, the jury, find the first named defendant, Vincent Petrenko, not guilty."

A collective gasp echoes throughout the room. Judge Jackson glares across the gallery. I drop my head as my heart sinks.

He continues. "In the second count of child endangerment, we, the jury, find the defendant, Vincent Petrenko, guilty."

My head pops back up as a softer gasp rolls through the room. I want to erupt in celebration, but I settle for a low fist pump.

"In the third count of contributing to the delinquency of a minor, we, the jury, find the defendant, Vincent Petrenko, not guilty."

Someone behind me whispers, "This is insane!"

I risk a glance at Aimee. She buries her face in her hands.

"In the fourth count of bribery of a public official, we, the jury, find the defendant, Vincent Petrenko, guilty."

I enjoy another fist pump. Petrenko's face turns crimson.

"In the first count of cruelty to children, we, the jury, find the second named defendant, Brenda Jo Starnes, guilty."

Aimee glances at me with a pained half-smile.

Finally, some justice!

"In the second count of child endangerment, we, the jury, find the defendant, Brenda Jo Starnes, guilty."

I allow myself a double fist pump. Brenda slumps over, shoulders heaving.

"In the third count of contributing to the delinquency of a minor, we, the jury, find the defendant, Brenda Jo Starnes, guilty."

Thank You, God!

"In the fourth count of obstruction, we, the jury, find the defendant, Brenda Jo Starnes, guilty."

I catch several quiet sighs of relief nearby. Despite this victory, I brace myself for the final defendant.

The judge continues. "In the first count of cruelty to children, we, the jury, find the third named defendant, Carl Theodore Blackwell, guilty."

Tiny Tot scampers to stand at my side. His eyes wide and welling with crocodile tears, he searches my face as a wave of relief crashes over me. I want to yield to the release of weeping in gratitude, but the verdict isn't over.

"In the second count of child endangerment, we, the jury, find the defendant, Carl Theodore Blackwell, guilty."

Carl continues to stare at the floor unmoving. I cannot hold back a huge smile.

"In the third count of contributing to the delinquency of a minor, we, the jury, find the defendant, Carl Theodore Blackwell, not guilty."

What?! That's not possible.

The woman seated to my right starts to cry.

"Steady, Danny," says the Bossman. "Buck up. You're fine."

"In the fourth count of bribery of a public official, we, the jury, find the defendant, Carl Blackwell, not guilty."

Aimee darts out of the room. I desperately want to follow. Rage blossoms in my gut as Brody begins to move toward me.

No, Brody! You can NOT fight in here! Maybe later, somewhere else, but not right now!

Clenching and unclenching my fists, I close my eyes and blow out several hard, deep breaths.

God, how is this justice? How is this fair? I thought You said You loved me and that You would defend me!

A gentle message flowed through my mind. "Danny, when you were saving Carl's life, did he deserve to die that day?"

YES!! A thousand times yes!

"But you allowed your heart to feel My heart for just a moment, and even though he didn't deserve it, you did what was right. You did what I would have done."

I'm sure wishing now that I hadn't! He's getting away with it!

"How much have you gotten away with?"

My face flushes and I cross my arms. I have no answer.

"Is My will always done on the earth, Danny?"

I recall the uncomfortable but revelatory discussion with Marti about God's will. New pain and injustice swirl through my heart. *Yeah, so? You want me to have faith and trust in You when You let child abusers and sickos do what they did to so many kids? He deserves to be put away for life! He actually deserves to burn! HOW IS THAT FAIR?!*

"It isn't fair at all, Danny."

The gentle tenderness in God's expression of His answer takes my breath away.

"Danny, you may not believe this, but I'm more angry about this than you are."

Wait, You... You get angry about the stuff that happens here?

God's soft, gentle kindness continues to disarm me. "Yes, My son. I absolutely get angry. I've been angry many times at the things that were done to you."

I bristle, surprised at my offense. *So if You were so angry about all of that, why didn't You DO something about it?!*

"You'll understand more in the future, but know this. I gave control of the earth to man, and through his will, man shifted that control to the enemy. He continues to steal, kill, and destroy. And even with all you went through, Danny, I've never once broken My promise to always be with you. And now I'm inviting you to trust Me, My precious son."

I have no idea what that looks like.

I want to dig deep into this conversation, but the banging of a gavel jolts me back to the courtroom where chatter and confusion are breaking out.

Judge Jackson addresses the gallery. "Order in the court!" The din falls to a quiet hush. "Counsel, we will reconvene exactly three weeks from today at 9:00 a.m. for the sentencing phase. The defendants are remanded to Fayette County Detention Center to await sentencing. Jury, you are dismissed. Thank you for your service. Court is adjourned."

As I stand up in a swirling stupor and inch toward the doors, Brody and Tiny Tot join me on either side. They want a good fight and a good cry. But my mind and my heart struggle in confusing disagreement with them as a simple phrase rolls around in my head.

God just called me His precious son.

32

AGE FORTY-NINE

A chilly, late-November breeze tousles my hair and blows at the pages of the journal under my hand. Sitting under the propane heaters outside at the Bluegrass Café with my favorite Americano, I hunch over the lines as my thoughts pour out through my pen.

Danny's thoughts: Lord, You said a thousand times that You were a God of justice. You told the story of the unjust judge who gave in to the incessant pleading from a poor widow. And You've said You're my defender and my victorious warrior. But from where I sit, it doesn't feel like any of that is true. Not only did Carl skate through a pathetic half conviction last month when everyone on the planet knows he's guilty, his sentencing is even more of a joke. This hurts!

My therapist said to name my emotions as I process, so here I go. Betrayed. Furious. Disgusted. Disappointed. And so much injustice. There's nothing fair about this.

Sitting back, I reread my words. This new practice of intentionally attempting to name, feel, and acknowledge my own emotions makes me want to run away. At least it isn't all roiling around in my gut. Kendra stands in her usual spot, waiting to record any evidence against me.

A familiar voice breaks into my mental gymnastics.

"Oh, hey, Mr. Pierce. How you doing?"

Smiling and healthy, Aimee Dixon shifts on her feet next to my table. Closing my journal, I jump up to give her a big squeeze. "Wow, it's so good to see you! How was your Thanksgiving?"

She brushes back a few locks of her pastel pink tresses. "You know, it was the best Thanksgiving I've had since I can remember. Nobody got drunk or high or started throwing hands. We actually played games and everybody was in the kitchen helping each other and laughing. It was perfect."

"That sure does sound perfect. What are you doing over this way?"

"Just came from my final emancipation visit in the judge's chambers. It's official! Signed and filed and everything! Even better, they agreed to my petition to change my name from Dixon back to Joyner to match my birth certificate!" Aimee's smile consumes her entire face. "Just wanted to grab some coffee and a snack before I head off to work."

I pull the chair out across from me and motion for her to join. "Come have a seat and catch me up!"

Unwrapping her scarf, she scoots the chair in and takes a long breath. "Gosh, okay, let's see. The biggest news is about that art competition you sponsored me for. Remember the one from the gallery in Little Five Points that was gonna take like a year to get through?"

"Oh yeah, the contest that came with a job," I answer with a nod.

Her face lights up even more. "I WON! Can you believe it?" Pumping both fists in the air, she dances and wiggles in her seat. "I start the new job next Monday! In a REAL gallery!"

"Aimee, that's absolutely fantastic! Good for you! So what'll you be doing?"

She shrugs, still smiling. "There's a good bit of grunt work, but that's to be expected. Cleaning. Taking care of inventory. Helping to process orders for shipping, stuff like that. But the best part is they have art classes on a regular basis, and I get to work directly with the kids' groups. We'll get to use all kinds of mixed media, work with clay. It's gonna be lit! Plus they said that once a quarter, employees can display their own work for sale. Can you imagine that? Selling something I actually painted!"

My heart nearly bursts with fatherly pride for Aimee as the memory of her sullen, tired face from our first meeting at school comes to mind. Leaning forward with a broad smile, I nod. "Wow, this is incredible. I'm so proud of you! I can see how excited you are. This sounds like it has the potential to drastically change your life."

The familiar purple-haired server stops by to take Aimee's order just as my stomach begins to rumble. Aimee opts for the caramel latte and a cream cheese croissant, and I add an everything bagel and a coffee refill for myself.

As the server breezes off, Aimee points to my journal. "Whatcha writing?"

A slight blush creeps up my neck as I lay my hand over the book. "Nothing much. I've been having some meaningful therapy sessions lately, and I've been hearing I need to be more honest with myself and with God about my emotions."

She snickers. "Don't we all?"

"Yeah, we all definitely do, that's for sure. I mean, you know what it's like growing up in survival mode. There's no time or place for emotions. So in a way it's like I'm learning a new language. I fought it at first, the concept of sitting and reflecting on what specific emotions are connected to a specific situation. It felt pretty girly, no offense."

She laughs and shrugs. "None taken. Guys and girls are wired different."

"Yes, they are. But it's been interesting how writing it all down actually does seem to be helping. The mental gymnastics that can spiral out of control for hours, the hypersensitivity and the quick-tempered reactions to just normal everyday life... those things are a lot less frequent since I started doing this kind of journaling on purpose."

Aimee's eyebrows rise. "Really? Huh, maybe I should try that."

Our server drops off our food and we dig in. As I'm several bites into my bagel, a clear thought passes through my mind. "Tell her the whole truth about Carl, Danny."

Pausing mid-chew, my eyes are drawn to where the small burn scars rest on my forearm just under my hoodie sleeve.

God? I think that's You. Are You serious? Tell her right now?

The response is instant. "Yes, Danny. She needs to know."

Wiping my hands and washing down the bagel with a long swig of Americano, I lean forward. "So, I have a strange question for you."

She side-eyes me. "Okay?"

"Do you believe in God?"

"That's not a strange question. At least I don't think it is.

And sure, I believe in God. Simon's whole family goes to church on Sunday. Since I moved in with his aunt Louise, I've been going to church with them nearly every weekend if I'm not working."

"Do you think someone is crazy if they say that God told them something?"

Propping her elbow on the table and her head on her hand, Aimee looks up and around as she thinks. "If you'd asked me that a few years ago, I'd have said they were definitely crazy. But no, I wouldn't say that now. I mean, if you tell me God said that you would sprout wings if you tried to jump off of the Empire State Building, then yes, that would be crazy." She grins. "God didn't tell you to do that, did He?"

I snicker. "Ha, nope, nothing like that."

We both laugh at her loud sigh of mock relief.

Pulling up my sleeve, my fingers trace lightly over the burn scars on my arm. "Do you remember the first day you came into my office and I showed you these marks?"

Aimee quickly moves her hands out of sight and under the table to keep her own arms from view. Her shining joy darkens to a frown. "Yeah?"

"How would it make you feel to know that the person who put these scars on my arm is the very same one who did that to you?"

Jaw dropped and eyes wide, Aimee looks closely at my upturned forearm.

Three cigarette burn circles in the shape of a triangle.

Slowly pulling up her sleeve, she brings her arm up to the table and lays it next to mine.

The scars are identical.

She shakes her head and stammers. "But... when... how... I don't understand. How is this possible?"

Sitting up and lowering my sleeve, I take a deep breath. "Butch and Gina Blackwell were my foster parents. I was placed in their home when I was about four. They had a teenage son with red hair. Can you guess what his name was?"

She can barely whisper the reply. "Carl."

"He followed in his father's footsteps with the foster care system because they figured out how much money they could make. As soon as he was legal, he got licensed. Been fostering ever since. I have no idea how many kids he's had come through his home. Many dozens, I'm sure. Makes me sick to think about it. I actually ran into one of Carl's other foster kids while I was in JDC. Same exact scar. I didn't completely make the connection with you though until I was working on your file at school."

Realization dawns across her face. "Wait, you knew even while the trial was going on and everything?"

I nod.

"So why weren't you included in the case testimony, like the stories from your own past? I mean, our scars are identical, that should mean something, right?"

Shaking my head, I flatten my palms on the table. "The statute of limitations ran out a long time ago for me. None of it would have been admissible in court. We could have had twenty people lined up who were hurt by Carl as kids, every single one of them with the same scar. Wouldn't have mattered. Your testimony hadn't passed that time limitation yet."

"That's really stupid."

"It most definitely is. But it's the way the law is written."

Clasping her hands on the table, she looks off toward the horizon as she takes a deep breath. "So knowing what you knew, how could you save Carl's life?"

Sitting back, I cross my arms. "How could you possibly know that?"

Her eyes drop. "You're not mad at me, are you?"

"No, not at all. Sorry if that's how it sounds. I just had no idea that anyone else saw me."

"Simon and I like to take his dog, Pringles, to the woof walk there at the North Elkhorn River. We had just let Pringles into the run when we heard the crash. We stood there at the fence and watched the whole thing. You walked by and I called you, but you just kept walking. I realized it was Carl when they wheeled the gurney right past us. But we thought it was weird that you didn't stay and talk to the police or anything."

Hands in my lap, I stare at my thumbs until the silence pushes me. "I didn't want to save him," I admit.

"Then why did you? I probably wouldn't have."

"Because God talked to me in that moment," I say with a shrug. "God asked me if I'd want to die that way, and what if this were me, what would that do to my wife. Trust me, I was still furious. But I did what I felt like God wanted me to do." I pat the top of my journal. "I've had lots to say about it to God since then."

"Okay. So you're talking to God about it. What's He saying back to you?"

I sigh. "Mostly that vengeance belongs to Him like it says in the Bible. And He says there are things I can't possibly know this side of heaven, and I'll understand it one day. But

He also says that He is still a God of justice, and that I can trust Him to keep His word."

She considers my answer in silence.

"He's also campaigning to get me to believe that He loves me unconditionally," I add. "I still have a lot of questions about that."

Dropping our checks on the table, the server grabs our empty dishes and heads toward the kitchen inside. I grab both of the bills before Aimee can get a hand on hers. "My treat," I answer. She tries to protest as I hold up a hand. "Consider it a congratulatory snack."

Gathering our things, we stand and exchange a hug.

"I'll have to check out that youth program at the gallery," I offer. "Maybe I could bring my kiddos."

She lights up again. "I'd love that!" She considers me for a moment and adds, "Mr. Pierce, I don't think I've ever known anybody who would do what you did because God told them to. I'm still going to my church with Simon, but if you ever start up a Bible study or something, I might be interested. I'm not sure I agree with God all the time. But I'm glad that God talks to you."

So am I.

33

AGE FORTY-NINE

M arti's counseling office is more comfortable after several visits. Even the faded paisley rug is starting to grow on me. Ever patient and faithful, Grace sits next to me and squeezes my hand with a peaceful smile. "I'm so proud of you, sweetie. Isn't it so cool what God is doing? I just love watching Him work. It never gets old."

Nervous tension mixed with curiosity swirls through my mind. I chug an entire bottle of water in an attempt to focus. It doesn't work; I've dribbled a stream down the center of my flannel shirt. My cheeks flushing, I grab several tissues to dry up the spill somewhat.

Marti is bright-eyed and energized. After draining her coffee mug, she moves it to the table behind her and she picks up the dry-erase board leaning against the leg of her filing cabinet. She lays the board across the desk in front of her. "So today we want to address the generational stuff that you've inherited. But before we dig into that, I'd love to hear your take on what you think 'generational sin' actually is from a biblical or spiritual perspective. How would you define it?"

"Well," I start, clasping my hands behind my head. "I'm not totally sure what my answer would be. I mean, I do think that those people are wrong who say that we're somehow accountable for what our ancestors did. Jesus handled all sin at the cross, right? The Bible says He took on the sin of the whole world. You just have to believe in what Jesus did, and trust in Him for salvation, and try to be better than your own parents were."

I glance quickly at Grace, hoping she agrees with me as I turn back to Marti and continue. "We obviously don't want to fall into repeating the same behaviors of our parents, so it's up to us to work hard at being more like Jesus. You know. Don't sin, tithe ten percent, all that stuff."

Marti nods to the open Bible on the front of her desk. "Danny, would you mind reading a couple of verses for me, please? It's already open to the right page. Just read Exodus chapter 20, verses 4 and 5."

I unclasp my fingers and pull the Bible into my lap. "You shall not make for yourself an idol, or any likeness of what is in heaven above, or on the earth beneath, or in the water under the earth. You shall not bow down to them or serve them, for I the LORD your God am a jealous God, visiting the iniquity of the fathers on the children to the third and the fourth genera-tion of those who hate me."

My brows furrow as I glance at the chapter heading.

The Ten Commandments

Replacing the Bible, I sit back. "Huh," is all I can say.

"Did you know this verse was actually within the Ten

Commandments, written by the finger of God himself?" asks Marti.

Grace and I answer together. "Nope."

"Seems kinda harsh," I add.

Marti tilts her head with a quizzical grin. "So one of the first questions we should ask ourselves is, why don't we know that this verse about things passing three and four generations is actually contained in the Ten Commandments? I was raised in a mainstream evangelical denomination. Our family was there every single time the doors were open, at least four times a week. I have never *not* been an active member in a church somewhere. But I was forty-five years old before I learned that this particular verse was located here. I wonder why that is?"

She lets the question hang unanswered in the air as she pulls a laminated page from a file sorter behind her. A color graphic of a genealogical family tree with multiple ancestry branches fills the page.

"So the first thing this verse tells us is that we definitely are impacted by generational sin. If you were to complete a traditional family tree like this one, just with your own biological parents, and you go back four generations on both sides and count up every bloodline ancestor, that is a minimum of thirty different people whose spiritual baggage rolls right down to you. And it doesn't matter whether you knew them or not."

My eyebrows shoot up. "Yikes."

"And unfortunately for you, Danny, we also have to add in every parental figure who exercised parental authority over us. Because when we come under their authority in our childhood, their spiritual garbage is imparted to us. So you also have foster parents and adoptive parents and other caregivers in the mix."

I cross my arms. "I don't know... I find that kinda hard to swallow. Like I can't blame my dad or my grandma for the situations I got myself into. I mean, I made those choices without their influence. Doesn't it mean that I'm trying to get a pass if I'm blaming someone I don't even know?"

"Have you ever heard of something called the Dutch Hunger Winter?" Marti asks.

"Nope."

Marti sits forward. "So, way back during World War Two, starting in late 1944, there was a village in the Netherlands that was totally cut off because of Nazi blockades, and the roads into this village were destroyed. Nothing could go in or out, no supplies, no food, absolutely nothing. Then that particular season, that area had the worst winter they'd seen in decades. So this entire village was literally starving. They were even eating things like grass and shoe leather and tulip bulbs just to stay alive. It took until May of the next year before the roads were finally restored, but 20,000 people died in that one area in that one winter."

Grace and I both groan in pained disbelief.

"And so you have this isolated people group that ended up becoming the subject of all kinds of scientific and medical studies in the years that followed. Through those studies it was proven scientifically that the women who were pregnant during that winter actually passed the effects of that trauma onto their unborn babies, and the physical effects continued into the grandchildren. Obviously there were a lot of underweight births and other direct physical impacts from the starvation. But those physical issues went on for generations.

Apparently, trauma that happens in the early months of pregnancy, when a baby is growing and changing so much, can affect that baby for the rest of their life. And those effects can even be passed down to future generations."

"Wow, that's kind of nuts," I say.

"Have you ever heard of epigenetics?" She continues.

"I mean, I know what genetics means, like our genes in our DNA."

"The word 'epi' means 'to sit on top of,'" Marti explains. "So epigenetics is referring to these switches that sit on top of our genes that turn different things on or off. Like my switch for blue eyes is turned off, and my switch for brown eyes is turned on. Behavioral epigenetics is this study of how different behaviors and things like trauma have a measurable impact on the switches. You can find an article from over ten years ago in *Discover Magazine* that lays out all of these examples. Survivors of massacres, children of violent or alcoholic parents, it's like there's this residue left behind on their DNA. And it's passed down literally in the blood. So we don't just inherit things like height and eye color. We inherit behavioral tendencies for things like anxiety and depression. Remember that scripture says, first comes the natural, then comes the spiritual."

I look at Grace. "You ever heard anything like this?"

She shakes her head, shoulders shrugging. "When I had my healing prayer time last month, they mentioned generational baggage a little bit, but nothing at all to this level."

Marti continues. "Therapists and counselors have a label to describe this. It's called 'destructive family patterns.' And what family on earth doesn't have some kind of destructive pattern? Lying, cheating, gluttony, abandonment, addiction, laziness – we all have something that our family has partnered with. Your family has different patterns than my family, but we all have them, right?"

I chuckle. "That's an understatement."

"And we just talked about what the scientific community calls it, either genetics or epigenetics. But scripture has a specific word for this. It's the Hebrew word for iniquity. If you dig into the original Hebrew, the word 'iniquity' actually refers to ancestral or bloodline sin. The Hebraic text is literally translated as 'a crook or bend in the line.' So every time you see this word 'iniquity' in the Old Testament, this is what it's referring to."

Mouth slightly agape, I'm unsure of what to do with all the revelation I've just heard.

Marti adds, "This is why we want to deal with all of this baggage we've inherited through all of the bloodlines that have had influence over us. In scripture, Daniel did this very thing in the book of Daniel in chapter nine. He stood up and repented for the entire nation of Israel."

"Wow, I never thought of it like that," says Grace.

"Yep," Marti answers. "Ezra chapter nine, same thing. Nehemiah chapter nine, same thing. So if it was good enough for them, it's good enough for us."

She lifts the dry-erase board we previously filled in and props it up on her lap. "So here are the names that we came up with for your bloodline in our first meeting together." She points to each name as she reads. "We have Nicholson. Rawlins. Eddie. Big Nana. Blackwell. Pierce. Leona. And then we need to add Grace's maiden name here because you married into it."

"It's McCroy," Grace answers. She spells it out letter by letter as Marti writes.

"Is that every name?" Marti asks. "Have we left anyone out who ever had any kind of parental or supervisory or care-giving responsibility over you before you turned eighteen?"

Sadness and self-pity mingle in my gut as I look over the list of names. Kendra writes furiously in the corner. Garrison stands next to her at attention, focused on me, frowning.

I take a moment to ponder. "No, that's everyone," I finally say.

"Now it's important to understand that this process isn't to dishonor or condemn anyone. We are doing what's called appropriating the blood of Jesus. We are applying what Jesus did on the cross, and we're separating you from what was imparted to you. Some people call this identificational repentance, which is exactly what Daniel did in the Bible."

I breathe deeply with a nod.

"Okay, Danny, I'm going to ask you to repeat after me. 'Jesus, I repent.'"

Wait, what? Repent?

"Hold up," I say. "I'm repenting? I thought this was about all of them. What am I repenting for exactly?"

Marti leans in. "We're repenting for the sins of the fathers the same way Daniel repented on behalf of all of Israel. Daniel wasn't personally responsible for what his ancestors had done, but he absolutely was suffering as a direct result of their sinful choices. It impacted the entire nation. And remember that 'repent' means to change our mind to align with the mind of God about a matter. So we're agreeing that our ancestors apparently did not repent for their sin, and we're standing up to identify with their bloodline and declare that

from today forward, we're agreeing with God about everything that's happened."

Opening my mouth, no sound will come out.

"Calm down, man," says the Bossman, annoyance dripping from every word. "Just spit it out. You're fine. Get it
over with."

I clear my throat. "Jesus, I repent."

Marti continues. "On behalf of the Nicholson bloodline."

My face flushes and my heart starts to pound. "On be…
on behalf…" I shake my head and force a light cough. "On
behalf of the Nicholson bloodline."

"The Rawlins bloodline."

The moisture in my mouth disappears. "The Rawlins
bloodline."

"Eddie's bloodline."

I nod. "Eddie's bloodline."

"Big Nana's bloodline."

Another nod. "Big Nana's bloodline."

Marti's voice softens. "The Blackwell bloodline."

Nope!

Rage shoots through me. I try to form the words as my
tongue is captured by injustice.

"Take your time," Marti offers gently.

I blow out another hard breath and force the words
through gritted teeth. "The Blackwell bloodline."

Marti continues. "The Pierce bloodline."

Why am I the one repenting?!

"Stop being such a baby, Danny!" the Bossman chides.
"Spit it out, man!"

I told you not to call me that!

I look up at Marti. "I don't know that this one is possible

to be completely honest. Do you have any idea how hard it is to think about repenting for everything they did to me?" Tiny Tot steps out to stand in front of Kendra, a tear already rolling down one of his cheeks.

"Danny," Marti answers, "I actually do understand how hard it is. Some of what happened to you actually happened to me. Did it feel fair for me to repent on behalf of the people who abused me? Absolutely not. But did it release me from the evil residue that was put upon me? Absolutely yes."

Anguish and pain threaten to flow from my eyes, so I squeeze them shut. Bracing myself, I force a response. "The Pierce bloodline."

Marti continues. "Leona's bloodline."

An ounce of pity surprises me as I repeat. "Leona's bloodline."

"And the McCroy bloodline."

I nod. "And the McCroy bloodline."

Marti leads. "Jesus, I repent for everything that these families have ever done."

Tiny Tot comes to stand beside me as my own tears begin to form. "Jesus... Jesus..." I force myself to sit up straight. "Jesus, I repent for everything that these families have ever done."

"I confess the sins of my ancestors."

I recoil at the emotional slap. "Why am I confessing the evil they all did? I didn't do those things!"

Marti is firm but tender. "Just like the Daniel of the Bible confessed the iniquity of his ancestors, we're identifying the sin that has happened in our bloodline and we're agreeing that what they did needs to be confessed. No one has confessed to all the sin that the families before you have committed. So by taking this position, you're saying that it formally stops with you. Scripture says if we confess our sin, He is faithful to forgive our sin, right?"

My shoulders slump, but I continue. "I confess the sins of my ancestors."

"I want no part in the sins or the curses of my ancestors."

I straighten a little, impressed at the empowerment in this phrase. "Lord, I want absolutely no part in the sins or the curses of my ancestors. Not one single bit."

Marti continues leading. "I forgive and release every one of these bloodlines."

Hard nope.

My head jerks up and my cheeks flush. "I'm supposed to forgive what they've done? I mean, you've heard some of the harm they did. It's unforgivable."

"Forgiving isn't saying it was good or right, Danny." Marti's compassion and tenderness are unexpectedly disarming. "None of it was good or right. It's the statement that we're nailing the list of their offenses to the cross in the same way that Father God nailed our list of offenses to the cross. It's releasing the power of what happened, and agreeing that because we have been freed of our debts, we choose in obedience to release others from their debts with us. Forgiveness isn't a feeling, Danny. It's the decision to let God be God."

Let God be God. I can be on board with that.

I stare at the floor for a moment. "Okay, can you repeat that last prayer part again, please?"

"I forgive and release every one of these bloodlines."

I close my eyes. "I forgive and release every one of these bloodlines."

"All the way back to Adam."

That's interesting.

"All the way back to Adam," I repeat.

"I release my ancestors to the cross of Jesus Christ," Marti continues.

Another tear rolls down my cheek. "I release my ancestors to the cross of Jesus Christ."

"I release all of my judgment, and I decree they owe me nothing."

But they DO owe me for what they put me through!

Tiny Tot puts one hand on my knee. Sniffing deeply, I clench my fists. "I release all of my judgment and decree… I decree…" Another tear escapes. "I decree they owe me nothing."

"I lay down my right for revenge and payback."

Sensing movement, I look toward Kendra and Garrison. Brody steps out from behind Kendra and cracks his knuckles. I cover my eyes with the heels of my hands. "I lay down my right for revenge and payback."

Marti says, "Lord, I repent for trying to sit in Your seat of judgment."

A guilty flush washes over me. "Lord, I repent for trying to sit in Your seat of judgment."

"And every demon transferred to me through these blood-lines," she continues.

Psh! Demons transferred? Okay, sure, whatever.

"And every demon transferred to me through these blood-lines," I answer.

"In Jesus' holy name I bind them, and I cast them to the pit."

I can get behind that.

"In Jesus' holy name I bind them, and I cast them to the pit."

She adds, "I now declare the blood of Jesus as my bloodline."

Whoa, that's a powerful statement.

I straighten again. "I now declare the blood of Jesus as my bloodline."

"I take my place as a son in the family of my Father God."

Son.

Sniffing hard, I stop to grab a tissue from the table in front of me and wipe at the tears beginning to erupt. "I take my place as a son in the family of my Father God."

"Now, Danny, you're going to ask the Lord a question, and He's going to give you some kind of response. It could be a word, or a sense, or a thought, or maybe a feeling or even a mental picture. So I want you to ask Him this question out loud: Jesus, what does this mean for me?"

Lifting up my chin, I swallow the sob that wants to escape. "Jesus, what does this mean for me?"

"Freedom," says a still, but very clear, small voice.

Opening my eyes, I glance around the room. Kendra and Garrison stand in the corner, both of them with arms crossed. Brody and Tiny Tot are gone for now. Grace and Marti smile at me as I find myself grinning.

"Well, I don't know if I'm making it up or if it's just my own thoughts, but I definitely heard the word 'freedom'."

The room is brighter and the colors are more vibrant than just a moment ago. I shake out my arms. "Whoa, I feel so much lighter! What's that about?"

Marti smiles. "We never know what kind of weight we've been carrying until it's gone."

Standing to extend the dry-erase board in my direction and handing me an eraser, Marti says, "Now I want you to erase every name written on this board."

Giggling with unexpected joy, I vigorously scrub every square centimeter. Relief and satisfaction flood me as the names of the past become a clean, empty slate.

Marti hands me a red dry-erase marker. "Now draw a big cross on the board."

I do as she instructs. A fresh gratitude springs up, pushing a couple of tears with it.

I wonder what freedom looks like for me.

34

AGE FORTY-NINE

I squeeze Grace's hand harder than I mean to. I'm thankful that she lets me.

Coming to Marti's office today, my knees are wobbly and my heart races more than normal, but I'm not sure why. After last week's prayer, I have a better understanding of how she's leading me to pray, and she's been nothing but kind and wise and full of truth. As Grace walks in with me now though, I sense something is different, like electricity and danger blended together. Nervous, uncomfortable energy flows from the Others like bulging powder kegs awaiting a single spark.

Decorated for Christmas, Marti's office has a lone, scraggly tabletop pine tree with a single red ball ornament and a baby blue tree skirt wrapped at its base. Smiling at the pitiful decoration, I'm reminded of the *Charlie Brown Christmas* television special that made such a sad tree famous.

Marti spends the first hour of our time today detailing what traumatic experiences do to the internal systems of the body and the brain. She draws diagrams on the dry-erase board and explains how scars are actually formed in the brain tissue through trauma. I've never heard this before. No one has ever shared the things Marti is sharing about how wounds and lies are planted by the enemy through trauma, whether emotional or physical. I've known for decades just how messed up I am. I've labeled myself crazy for years. But I've never considered that tangible, physical things going on inside of my body could actually have come from the abuse in my past. My mind reels at the revelation.

Picking up a small bottle of anointing oil from the shelf, Marti asks to pray over me about the traumas I experienced. Part of me wants to protest. The other part struggles not to weep as she traces the sign of the cross with oil on my forehead.

No one has ever offered to anoint me with oil as they prayed for me before. I recall reading something about this in the Bible, and I've seen it at Living Waters Chapel a few times. But it's never been done for me personally.

The Others do not like this. Their anger toward me is palpable.

As Grace lays one hand on my knee, Marti kneels on the ground before me and begins praying. "Danny, I speak in Jesus' name to every single part of you, spirit, soul, and body, that has ever carried the cellular memory of trauma."

My skin prickles at her words as I recall just a few of the traumatic things I've endured. Scenes of rage, violence, shame, and death swirl briefly. I inhale deeply, forcing myself to listen as she continues, emphasizing every word.

"I speak to your eyes that saw traumatic sights, defiling sights, and unwanted sights. I speak to sights of terror and violence, and sights of danger and rejection."

Tears begin to slowly fall, but I am mesmerized by this prayer. In rare form, I willingly let them fall.

Marti continues, her voice tender yet determined. "Danny, I speak to your ears that have heard traumatic sounds, sounds of defilement, and sounds of danger. I speak to terrifying noises, and to threatening and dangerous words."

The tears flow more heavily now as auditory memories rush by. The dark laughter of my foster parents. Carl's sadistic voice. My dad's raging. The gunfire that killed my cousin Frankie. My own voice crying out in agony. A soft whimper escapes my lips.

"I speak to every part of your physical body," Marti prays. "I speak to the skin, bones, muscles, tissue, ligaments, and joints, every single part of your physical body that has ever been on the receiving end of unsafe or unwanted touch, violent or painful touch, defiling touch, and the parts of you that carry the cellular memory of injuries."

A sob escapes me as my shoulders jerk. I bite my lip to regain control. Marti waits a moment before continuing.

"Danny, I speak to the inward parts of you that have carried the emotional weight of trauma. I speak directly to the anxiety that rests like a rock in the gut. I speak to the racing mind, the rapid heartbeat, the clenched fists and clenched jaw." Marti's voice grows stronger in authority. "I speak to every single one of these, and in the name and by the blood of Jesus Christ, the risen Messiah, I command every one of those things to leave you NOW."

I jump briefly, as with the word "now," Marti snaps her fingers. But she continues, ever so softly as she rises from kneeling and begins to use her hand to brush my shoulders off as if she were wiping away dust.

"Let it fall away," she says. "Let all of the trauma fall away, Danny. Just like sand falls off of you when you stand up from the beach, let every bit of this fall away." Marti continues brushing me off another moment as she prays, soothing yet commanding. "Trauma, you will leave now and never return. You're not allowed here anymore. You have to leave because Jesus Christ paid for Danny to be free of trauma. Jesus, I ask You to come with Your river of living water, and wash Danny from the top of his head to the soles of his feet, and every molecule in between. Lord, come and cleanse him of every single thing that the enemy has done, so those things can never impact him again."

Several more sobs wrack my body as a physical sense of shedding ripples across me. I'm shocked that I can actually feel the weight of something leaving me. I am unmistakably lighter.

Continuing to stand in front of me, Marti is silent as she allows me to weep. I'm a little surprised at my freedom to cry this much, but there is no shame here. Finding a moment to pause, I reach for a tissue.

"How are you doing?" asks Marti. "Doing okay?" I can only manage a nod and a half-smile. I dare not look at Grace. I fear if I speak or glance her way, I'll erupt again. I close my eyes.

Placing one hand gently on top of my head, Marti continues her prayer. "Danny, I speak to the soldier within you, the one who is walking in hypervigilance, the part of you that believes you have to be on alert at all times, constantly looking over your shoulder expecting danger. I thank that soldier for the job you've done to protect Danny. But your job is over. In Jesus' holy name, I command you, at-ease soldier, you are to stand down. You are relieved from duty. I declare to you Danny that you are free to stop looking for danger. I command hypervigilance to leave you and never come back. Jesus is your defender. He goes before you and behind you, and He is your victorious warrior, as it is written."

I slump forward under the supernatural release of pressure I sense through my body. It's as if I've been a puppet held aloft under tension, and someone has just severed every string. I almost wonder if I'm paralyzed.

Kneeling in front of me again, Marti's voice cracks a little as she fights her own flood of emotion. She declares. "I speak to tiny Danny, to elementary age Danny, to middle and high-school age Danny. I bless those parts of you that were stuck in trauma. I tell you that you're free now. It's over. There's no more danger. Danny is a grown adult, and he is owned by the Lord Jesus."

At this statement, I sit up slowly and inhale more deeply than I think I've ever breathed before. My lungs have an increased capacity, as if I'm hooked up to pure oxygen. Marti's words echo with power. I exhale and clear my throat.

"You said something just now that really impacted me," I say. I gaze at the rug to avoid eye contact, and I glance briefly at the clock on the wall, noticing that the time is 4:50 pm. "You said the words 'tiny Danny.' I'm not sure why, but there's something there."

Rising to take her seat again, Marti answers, "Absolutely. Let's minister to the tiny one inside you. I'm going to ask you to close your eyes again, and take a long, deep breath."

I sit back and breathe as she asked, then she continues. "Danny, can you picture yourself as that tiny Danny? Once you have a mental picture formed in your mind, share with me what you see."

An image immediately forms of me around four or five years old. I'm in the Blackwell's house where I lived with my sister. I'm pleasantly surprised that the usual fear and power-lessness I feel when I picture that season isn't there. I share with Marti, "Okay, yes. I can see myself. I'm about four, maybe five, and I'm in my foster home. Butch and his friends are all there, and so is Carl. Nothing is happening, but I can tell that little me is terrified."

"Excellent," she answers. "Now keeping your eyes closed, I'm going to ask you to see yourself now as a forty-nine-year-old Danny walking up to the front door of that house where the younger you is inside and is afraid. Can you see that?"

Rage and injustice begin to roil in my belly as the image of my adult self walking up to this house plays on the movie screen of my mind. I nod, my lips clamped shut into a thin, angry line.

Marti guides me. "I want you to see yourself opening the front door of that house, and walk into the room where the four-year-old you is there with the foster family. I want you to imagine yourself now, as an adult, walking over to your younger self. I want you to take his hand, and I want you to say this out loud to him."

I steel myself to follow her instructions. The physical pain in my heart at this scene with four-year-old me takes my breath away.

Rising to place a tender hand on my shoulder, Marti leads me. "Tiny Danny, I want you to know how sorry I am that all of that happened to you. It wasn't right, and you didn't deserve it."

Starting to repeat after her, anguish erupts in gasping sobs as I speak. I get to the part about telling tiny me that he didn't deserve it, and I protest. "But I DID deserve it! I heard that for years! I deserved everything I got!"

Ignoring my falsehood, Marti gently repeats her statement, intending for me to follow. "Tiny Danny, you didn't deserve it. No one deserves what happened to you."

I shake my head and force myself. "You didn't..." I inhale sharply. "You didn't... you didn't deserve it!" The words rush out with bitter tears.

Grace rubs my back gently as Marti continues. "It's not your fault. You were not responsible. Tell him that."

Shaking my head, I protest again. "But it WAS my fault! That's what they told me! Oh this hurts so bad! I can't!"

Unmoved, Marti repeats herself again, expecting me to follow. "Tiny Danny, none of this was your fault. You were not responsible. Your childhood was stolen from you. That's the truth, Danny."

Staring at the clock on the wall that now reads half a minute 'til 5:00 pm sharp, I use the clock's second hand as a mental countdown to propel myself to keep going. I have to shout the words to force them out as I fight against myself to accept truth. The seconds tick down, three, two, one. "It wasn't your fault! It wasn't your fault!"

"Very good," Marti says. "Now, you're still holding Tiny Danny's hand. Using your mind's eye, adult you is going to lead little you out of that house. Jesus is waiting for you both outside. See yourself walking tiny Danny out to Jesus, and I want you to say this to him as you leave. 'No one is going to hurt you anymore. Jesus is our protector now, and you're free to just be a little boy. You're safe now.' After you say this to him, Danny, I want you to tell me once both of you are out of the house with Jesus."

An unexpected boldness arises as I follow Marti's lead, speaking to little me as we leave that house of horror. In the movie screen of my mind, Jesus embraces both the younger me and adult me outside. His bearded face beams with compassion and tender comfort. The green of the grass, the warmth of the sun, and the shocking depth of love and safety pulse through my heart.

Unable to contain the flood, I erupt. A grievous, painful wail begins to roar from the very depths of my being. The lament resonating from within is almost otherworldly, as if multiple voices are raging all at once. But like the force of a dam surging through a breach, this tidal wave of excruciating pain leaving me cannot be stopped. And I don't want it to stop. I scream over and over as time seems to stand still. I've known my entire life that this deep well of pain was there, but it was always safer to keep it buried. Until now.

I scarcely notice how Marti prays over me just under her breath. Her words are unfamiliar gibberish, but somehow I sense overwhelming peace emanating through those sounds. Grace sobs quietly next to me. Though my own emotions are at the forefront, I am grateful for her compassion.

Oblivious to how much time passes, the flood of agony recedes as abruptly as it began, and my wailing fades out. Deep, cleansing breaths take the place of my cries, and I can enjoy the sensation of a full breath for perhaps the very first time in my life. I bask in the quiet calm, unfamiliar and mesmerizing. I have never experienced such stillness.

I want to stay in this place forever.

35

AGE FORTY-NINE

*A*m I dead up in heaven?

No, my knee is brushing up against my wife's leg, and the faint aroma of frankincense anointing oil lingers in the air. Leaning forward with my elbows on my knees and my eyes heavy, I slowly come into awareness of my surroundings. Euphoria envelops me. I'm completely content to just sit here.

"So," Marti begins softly. She waits a moment. "How are you doing, Danny?"

Inhaling deeply again, I allow my eyes to open. The brightness of the room momentarily blinds me. *Was it this bright when I came in here?*

Allowing my eyes to adjust, I lean back into the sofa cushion. I look over at Grace, her face red and her eyes still brimming with tears. She smiles sweetly as she dabs at her nose with a tissue, and I smile back. *Has she always been this beautiful?*

I turn slowly to where Marti is seated in front of her office window. The bare branches of the dogwood tree sway with the wintry breeze against a cloudless blue sky. I marvel at the beauty. A shocking realization slams into my heart as I gaze around the room.

The Others are gone.

Maybe they're just staying out of sight because they're still mad at me.

I squeeze my eyes closed and I think about Kendra, Garrison, Brody, and Tiny Tot. I expect them to be standing right in front of me as I open my eyes again. That's how it's always been.

There's no one here but Grace, Marti, and me.

I lean forward to look around Marti, expecting to find one of them hiding behind her. Nothing. I glance past Grace expecting the same thing. I see only the floor lamp, the open bookcase, and the Christmas manger scene figurines. My head is a swivel as I take in the entire room from corner to corner, expecting to see one of the Others camped out somewhere. But none of them are anywhere to be found.

Closing my eyes once more, I think about the voices of Kendra, Garrison, the Bossman, Brody, and Tiny Tot. My entire adult life, I've only ever had to think of their names and they would start a conversation. I open my eyes again. There's no voice but my own.

A new wave of tears begins to fall, but this time they are accompanied by laughter. Trying to compose myself, I look at Grace with wonder. I cannot believe the words coming from my own mouth. "They're... they're just gone. They're all gone, Grace. It's just me. Every one of them is gone."

Grace's jaw drops, her brows raised and tears instantly welling up. She can barely whisper, "What?!"

Laughing and crying again, I look directly at Marti. "You

CRAZY HAS A NAME

don't understand," I explain. "For as long as I can remember, every single time I have looked at someone like I'm looking at you right now, the part named Kendra was always standing just behind whoever I was looking at. She would be holding a clipboard, and she would be taking notes about everything I said or did." A teary giggle escapes me. "I'm looking right at you, Marti, and she isn't there."

A thrilling mixture of awe and relief washes over me.

But what if they come back when I walk out the door?

I look at Grace, my eyes pleading. "I don't want to leave this place, babe. What if they come back? I'm afraid they'll come back when we leave." Having tasted the elation of being free of the Others, desperation grows.

Marti leans forward. "Do I have your permission to take authority so they don't?"

Her question is barely complete before I blurt, "Absolutely!"

Looking toward the door, Marti points to something I cannot see. Her words are bold and resounding with supernatural power, and the room is electric. "I speak in the name and authority of the Lord Jesus Christ who lives in me, and I command every single one of you to leave and stay gone permanently! It is written that what I bind is bound, so in Jesus' holy name I bind every single one of you tormentors and I cast you to the feet of Jesus for Him to deal with you. Out! Your access to Danny is broken from this day forward, and you will never afflict him again. I declare for Danny, on earth as it is in heaven, that he is whole and in unity in his spirit and soul and body, as Father God created him to be."

Inhaling deeply, Marti turns back to me. "Lord Jesus, what

would you like to give Danny in exchange for what you've just taken from him?"

Closing my eyes, I giggle and tear up again as a mental picture forms immediately. Jesus and I are sitting side-by-side in my backyard on the stone bench again. His arm drapes over my shoulder in a brotherly touch. Smiling, I convey aloud the phrase I sense from Jesus. "He said, 'I'm going to teach you how to have fun again.'"

36

AGE FORTY-NINE

I am forty-nine years old, and I've never entered into worshipping Jesus the way I did in this morning's service.

Today is the Sunday before Christmas, and it's been a full four days since I walked out of Marti's office a radically changed man. I am awakened to the existence of life through every sense. Colors are brighter. Smells are richer. Sounds are infused with emotion and beauty. Loaded down laundry baskets are lighter, and I've had to stop myself from dancing and giggling more than once.

So this is what most other people feel like most of the time? This is what normal is? I like it.

The end-of-service church prayer line is more full and animated than usual. My cheeks flush at the awareness that I'm the reason for the celebratory fuss. But I cannot keep what the Lord has done for me a secret.

Our precious group of friends surrounds me along with many of the congregants who have just heard my miraculous story. Their hugs, triumphant tears, and joyful laughter blends with my own as they see the outside of the new me that I know is inside.

Pastor Glen creates an inner circle with his intercessory prayer team and we all join hands. Grateful tears well up as I take in the faces of people who have stormed heaven for me to contend for my healing, all while loving and honoring me in the messy meantime.

After Glen's beautiful prayer and many more tear-filled expressions of rejoicing in the miracle Jesus has performed, Grace slips her hand in mine and squeezes.

"Hey, before we head out, Claudia Fowler had something she wanted to share with us. She and Jim are back in the prayer room. She said it'll just take a minute. Josiah has Abigail in the arts and crafts center."

As I step in the now-familiar space where the gifted intercessory team has regularly laid hands on me over the past few months in prayer, a new wave of peace-filled wonder washes over me. Our friends Claudia and Jim stand up from the padded chairs and embrace me like a champion.

Grabbing my hand, Claudia pulls me to sit beside her. Jim and Grace join, the four of us in a close circle knee to knee. Claudia beams with excitement.

"Danny, I've been so excited to talk to you since Grace called me with the news Friday morning! I just had to tell you what the Lord showed me while I was praying for you. You're aware that Grace has been sharing with me whenever you've had your ministry sessions scheduled with Marti, just so we can be covering you in prayer while you're there. So last Wednesday morning I woke up with this prayer on my heart for you, and I wrote it down."

Claudia picks up a small moleskin journal from the side table next to her. She opens it and reads the entry.

"I lift Danny Pierce to You today, Jesus. Without You he is orphaned and lonely. I know Your spirit lives in him. Manifest Yourself over him. Come, Lord Jesus, as his teacher and guide in a powerful way. Do not leave him comfortless tomorrow night, during and after his ministry session with Marti. Jesus, come as the Comforter. Come to his heart to abide. Break all demonic forces that are fighting for his mind. I hold Your blood, Jesus, over Danny's mind, will, and emotions. Thank You in advance for what I know You can do. In Jesus' holy name, amen."

She turns the page to continue. "Then first thing Thursday morning as I prayed, I wrote this entry."

Claudia's voice breaks with a mixture of weeping and laughter as she reads her writing. "Danny was healed from his dissociative disorder. He is walking in freedom and fire! Thank You, Jesus, You broke all of them!"

Holding the page for me to see, she points to the multiple underlines of the last sentence before closing the book to lay it down.

He broke all of them!

The entry was dated and timed almost twelve hours before I was actually healed. I shake my head and start to answer, but she pats my knee.

"That's not even the best part. Thursday afternoon while you were in your ministry session, it was right at 5:00 p.m. I was still praying as I started to pull out the ingredients to make dinner. As I opened the fridge, in my mind I saw a picture of these massive, dark silver magnets next to one another. But they were opposing each other so they wouldn't stick together. Like the force of the resistance was massively powerful. But then all of a sudden, the magnets both flipped around and they slammed together and stuck to one another. It was almost like I could physically hear the banging together of the metal, and the force was so intense, it felt in my spirit like an explosion. And Danny, as God is my true witness, in that exact moment at 5:00 p.m, I absolutely knew you were healed. I heard God say in my spirit, 'It's done!' I actually fell to my knees in front of the fridge and began to cry with tears of joy."

5:00 p.m. The precise moment all of hell erupted out of my belly and vanished.

A grateful sob erupts as I glance at Grace. She giggles and weeps as she shakes her head. I want to reply, but I have no words.

Grace's voice is an awe-filled whisper. "Wow, Claudia. The Lord did it. Right then. He showed you what was happening inside of Danny's mind at the exact moment of his healing!"

Claudia brushes her tears away. "Isn't He so good?!"

A new wave of appreciation and thankfulness overwhelms me, but I don't resist. I welcome the tears as I see a mental image of Jesus in my own mind, His arms open toward me in an invitation.

Yes, Jesus. You are so, so good.

37

AGE FIFTY-ONE

I am fifty-one years old, and I am crazy.

Crazy for enrolling in seminary!

Standing on the back porch enjoying my coffee with the sunrise, I gaze in wonder at the beauty of the imperfect back yard. For most of my married life, the overgrown shrubs and the weeds erupting from the flower beds would have poked at me with urgency to deal with them so my neighbors wouldn't judge. My reality today is that it's just not that big of a deal.

I marvel at the journey of the last two years since the Lord healed and delivered me. Some days I still catch myself looking for Garrison or Kendra or Tiny Tot. Then I'm flooded again with gratitude and awe as I remember my wholeness. My mind drifts to last night's dinner table, everyone relaxed and smiling, all of us enjoying each other's company without wondering if I'm about to blow up or freak out. I am so incredibly blessed.

The Lord has also brought my sleeping dreams to life. I don't dream every night. But when I do, my dreams are crystal clear, filled with divine strategy or supernatural wisdom. I've dreamed of praying for a homeless man wearing an orange hat, and then I see that very man the next day at the gas station. I never saw myself as gifted enough to pray for other people. Now it's second nature.

The dreams about seminary were also crystal clear, and I'm so grateful to the Lord for giving dreams to Grace about that as well. When she and I had the exact same dream three separate times in a month, we both knew this was the Lord's plan.

Circling her arms around my waist to hug me from behind, Grace rests her cheek on my shoulder. "So, you ready for the big day?"

I place my coffee cup on the porch railing and pivot to wrap my arms around my wife. Cheek to cheek, we gaze at the sunrise together.

I take my time to answer, which is also a newly learned reality. "You know, I am ready. I'm pretty sure I'll be the oldest guy in the class by far. But I'm okay with that. I'm not there for them anyway. We both know this is where the Lord is calling us."

"Youth Pastor Danny," she says. "I just love the sound of that so much. I still can't believe Pastor Glen made that happen so quickly. I definitely did not have that on my bingo card!"

Stepping back, I turn Grace's chin to face me. "This calling will always be a calling for us both, not just a calling for me. I know I'm the one going to classes, but it's not about me. It's about how God wants to use us together. And I hope you know how incredibly grateful I am, for marrying me, for staying with me in the mess, and for always loving me. I love you so much, Grace Pierce."

She cups my cheek in the palm of her hand. "I love you, Danny Pierce. And I could not be more proud of you. Proud to be your wife, proud of the intentional father you've become, proud of you for listening to the Lord. I'm proud of you for trusting Him, and so incredibly proud of who He's making you to be."

I want to linger in this sweetness, but my phone alarm chirps. Time to head out for class!

The drive to the campus takes an easy twenty minutes, and after another ten minutes to park and walk to my first class, I slip into a vacant aisle seat near the front of the lecture hall. College students, young professionals, and a few older folks nod as they file into their own seats. I was right. I'm the oldest by far, almost old enough to be a father to some of these kids. I'm pleased at the deep sense of peace that covers me.

A wiry man who looks to be about my age hustles to the podium. His wild bed-head and wrinkled shirt scream typical professor. But joyful energy and light radiate from his face.

I already like this guy.

"Good morning, class. I'm Professor Cuttlering, but you can call me Cutty. Welcome to the first chapter of an incredible story!"

Grabbing a dry-erase marker, he writes on the whiteboard behind him in massive letters.

FAITH

"So, we're gonna jump right in. This class is about faith. I don't mean faith in Jesus Christ. That's pretty much a prerequisite for seminary, right?"

A few students chuckle.

Cutty leans over his podium and rests on his elbows, taking a moment to make eye contact with every student in the room.

"So, who has a personal example of the impact of faith in their life? Who wants to share?"

My hand shoots up as I rise from my seat. Cutty points at me.

Waving, I clear my throat. "Hi, my name is Danny Pierce. Boy, do I have a story for you!"

Dear beloved reader,

From the depths of my heart, thank you for taking the time to walk with Danny in his story of healing and freedom. It is my sincere hope that this book has challenged you, touched your spirit, and sparked a desire for more.

Reviews are critical to the sharing of this message to others, so I thank you in advance for taking a moment to write a review on Amazon, Goodreads, or other platforms where this book is available. I'd also be honored if you would recommend this book to your friends and family.

As mentioned in the author's note, my involvement in inner healing and deliverance ministry is what brought about stories like Danny's. Part of walking through this kind of heart work is learning how to pray in power and authority.

As a token of my gratitude for reading *Crazy Has A Name*, I invite you to download a powerful resource that has personally impacted me and thousands of others on the path to healing: the "Daily Spiritual Warfare Prayer". Adapted from an original prayer by Victor Matthews, this scripturally-based prayer has been an effective daily source of strength, identity, and authority for many years.

Follow the link below to download your complimentary "Daily Spiritual Warfare Prayer" and embark on your own journey toward identity and authority in Christ.

https://www.lambornauthor.ink/freecontent

Abundant blessings to you on your journey with Jesus!
Nanci Lamborn

MINISTRY RESOURCES

For any reader who may feel drawn to step into the same kind of inner healing prayer that Danny found so impactful, all of the below organizations are highly regarded for their ministries to the hurting and wounded.

May you experience your own breakthrough as you allow the Lord to lead you on your journey of healing.

- Bethel Sozo www.bethelsozo.com
- Christian Healing Ministries https://www. christianhealingmin.org/
- Elijah House www.elijahhouse.org
- Freedom in Christ www.ficm.org
- Orbis Prayer www.orbisprayer.org
- Restoring the Foundations www.restoringthe foundations.org

For more information about Mike Hutchings and his trauma prayer work, find Mike at The God Heals PTSD Foundation. This organization provides education, training, resources, and awareness events that equip and educate to give treatment and restoration to those who have experienced trauma that continues to impact their present lives. The Foundation also provides resources to chaplains, treatment centers, retreat centers for military veterans and active-duty soldiers, and organizations dedicated to support military and first responders. Find out more at www.godhealsptsd.com.

Angry Daughter: A Journey from Hatred to Love

Forty percent of us carry scars of abuse. Are you ready to break free?

Well into her mid-forties, Nanci Lamborn was a critical, angry Christian who carried a consuming hatred of her mom. Frustration, annoyance, and offended contempt were constant companions at every family gathering, and these emotions robbed Nanci of her inner peace for decades. With no concept of the freedom available, she surrendered to heart healing prayer and experienced profound transformation.

From navigating the messy relationship with her dramatic, difficult mom, to surviving traumatic abuse, and finally assuming the role as a caregiver before her mom's tragic death, Nanci's story blends gritty, uncomfortable truth with beautiful and tender healing.

Now as an ordained minister of inner healing, Nanci walks with hurting people to introduce them to the supernatural power of forgiveness, repentance, and release of the painful past to Jesus. Angry Daughter is Nanci's very personal journey down that same path to peace.

Part personal growth, part hilarious memoir, and part self-help, Angry Daughter thematically weaves its way through resentment and grief, to fear and shame, and from trauma to destiny. Nanci paves a clear pathway for those ready to begin their own journey of releasing Mom to the Lord in prayer.

Find *Angry Daughter* on Amazon, Google Play Books, and many other online retailers.